LOVE LETTERS FROM CUBA

A Novel

From the author of
Waiting on Zapote Street,
winner of the Latino Books Into Movies
Award, Drama TV Series category

Betty Viamontes

LOVE LETTERS FROM CUBA

Published in the United States by

Zapote Street Books, LLC, Tampa, Florida

Book cover by SusanasBooks LLC

Except for the testimonies, this book is a work of fiction. Any resemblance to actual locales or events or any persons, living or dead, is entirely coincidental.

ISBN: ISBN: 978 1-955848-05-3

Printed in the United States of America

Testimony

To Our Children and Grandchildren

We only ask that you love each other and your husbands or wives with the same immense love that united your father and me.

No matter what stones we found along the way, the obstacles, the unjust politics, the twelve years of separation, we stayed together until death.

This is our legacy to you. Love is the most beautiful feeling that exists in the world.

1964 – Our wedding

1997 – Year of your father's death (till death do us part)

This letter was written by Milagros Valdés, my mother. She left it for her children to discover it after her death.

Letters are like droplets of life, snapshots of moments that won't return.

I dedicate this book to—

My mother, for showing me that anything is possible.

My beloved husband and my family, for their unconditional support.

My loyal readers, for reading my books and encouraging me to keep writing.

Chapter 1

Paulo

While driving my metallic-blue 2020 CR-V, I felt acid rising in my stomach as I replayed my encounter with my cousin Marta the night before. Over wine and pasta at the quaint Italian restaurant Casa Santo Stefano, she had asked whether—now that I had ended my relationship with Paulo—she could go after him. I had noticed her attempts to seduce him at family gatherings before. Back then, I dismissed them. Now, I couldn't.

It was July 2021, in the middle of a pandemic that had claimed more than 600,000 lives in the United States alone. We were living in a world of masks, social distancing, and deep divisions that threatened to unravel life as we knew it. Yet that morning, it was Marta—not the virus—who occupied my thoughts.

I could see her as clearly as if she were sitting beside me in the passenger seat: leopard-print stretch jeans hugging her hips, a black low-cut top revealing her ample bosom, high heels clicking against the restaurant's tiled floor. Her long red nails flashed as she gestured, and I could almost smell her heavy, flowery perfume while she talked incessantly about her clients at the beauty salon.

Why did I agree to go out with her? I had asked myself that question all evening.

When the waiter brought the check, she glanced at it and gently nudged it toward me, the faintest crinkle of a smile playing at her lips. I said nothing and paid the entire bill—eighty dollars with the tip—money that left a noticeable dent in my budget during a time of rising prices.

And here I was, delivering food to my grandfather—as I did most Sundays—while allowing my insecurities to consume me.

My mother insisted he didn't need my help. A wounded veteran who had retired from Tampa General Hospital as a security officer, he received a pension, and his house was fully paid off. I would tell her he was living on a fixed income and that if I chose to spoil him, that was my decision. What I didn't tell her was that, for as long as I could remember, I had felt a special bond with him.

When I was little, he took me out for ice cream and taught me how to defend myself. For my seventh birthday, he gave me a mid-sized brown teddy bear with a blue bow—one I still keep. It wasn't the best gift I received that year, but the joy in his eyes as he watched me unwrap it told me something far more valuable: few people would ever love me the way he did. After I turned twelve, he began taking me to the shooting range. Those outings ended abruptly when my mother found out.

Now I am twenty-four, two years out of the University of South Florida with a business degree, and lonelier than I had ever been. The daughter of Cuban parents who had raised me as though we still lived on the island—with chaperones and rigid rules—I had finally tasted freedom after graduation. I rented a small apartment in trendy Hyde Park, conveniently located near shops and restaurants. It wasn't large, but it was mine.

Only months after I moved in, life around me came to a halt when the pandemic struck. Overnight, businesses shut their doors, people retreated into their houses, and telecommuting became the norm for many offices, mine included.

My roommate moved out after the one-year lease ended. At the time, Paulo asked me if I wanted to move in with him to his condo in Hyde Park instead of renewing my lease. That would have helped me save money, especially now that rents were so high and mine had increased by over 10%, a significant amount considering I was no longer sharing my apartment with anyone. However, knowing that living together would have escalated his volatile relationship with my parents, I declined.

Paulo

Paulo had asked me to marry him in 2020, on the day after Thanksgiving. I told him I needed more time to get my parents ready.

Then, the breakup came at the end of June 2021.

Tensions had flared up at home, and my mother stopped concealing her disapproval of Paulo. She rolled her eyes when he spoke about his life in Brazil, and during our last two visits, she started showing him pictures of Mark and me dancing together during my *quince* (sweet fifteen) celebration. I could see Paulo glancing at me as my mother continued to turn the pages of the album, full of photographs. His eyes begged me to say something. I didn't.

I came to realize that nothing I could do would change anything. He simply didn't meet my parents' standards. He wasn't Cuban, he wasn't a professional, and he didn't want a family.

Three strikes, and you're out.

Those were the reasons I used to justify the breakup. Yet nothing is ever that simple.

We had been together for three years. He didn't have a college education, but he, an immigrant from Brazil, was passionate, hardworking, and—like my grandfather—accustomed to hardship. It impressed me that in only a few years after his arrival in the United States, he had built his own kitchen cabinet company from the ground up.

So why did I walk away from him now? Was it because of my parents' nagging? I knew who he was from the beginning. Did I suddenly believe he was not good enough for me? How could I think that someone with the work ethic, determination, and kindness of my grandfather was not worth fighting for? Perhaps if I had lived a fraction of my grandfather's difficult life, I would feel different. As he often said, "Hardship strengthens the human spirit."

I didn't want to behave like the typical Cuban princess whose parents had given her so much that she had lost touch with reality. Not that I was Cuban. Like my mother, I was born in Tampa. My father came from Cuba during the Mariel boatlift in 1980 after being part of the thousands of people who flooded the Peruvian Embassy in Havana to request political asylum. I was thankful to my parents for wanting me to experience the best life they could afford.

My quince birthday party, held at the Columbia Restaurant in Ybor City, made me feel like I was on top of the world: Spanish dancers, paella, and ten girls who looked like bridesmaids wearing long, peach fluffy dresses and dancing with boys in tuxedos, and me at the center in a white dress that would have resembled a wedding gown if it had not been for my red gloves. That night, I danced with Mark, a Cuban boy, one whom my parents approved.

As all the couples danced to old Cuban songs and a waltz, pleasing our guests with well-executed choreographies, we resembled the aristocrats of Cuba's past.

Ybor City also had a special meaning for me. The historic neighborhood northeast of downtown Tampa, Florida, had contained a little portion of Cuba since 1956, when a tiny park, known as José Martí Park—located on 8th Avenue—was donated by Tampa to the island. A marker in the park describes how, in 1893, Paulina Pedrosa, a then-resident of the area, had offered refuge to assassination target José Martí, Cuba's poet, patriot, and "Apostle of Freedom."

Having my coming-of-age party held in this historic city with close ties to Cuba made me feel connected to the land of my father and my grandfather.

My parents also gave me a Catholic, private school education, a closet full of pretty dresses and shoes, and large family gatherings. Those became much less frequent after I reached my teenage years, as children grew up and moved away to other cities in search of the perfect job. Little by little, our large Cuban family had blended itself almost out of existence. Even my cousins had married Anglo-Saxon men and had American children with little or no connection to our Cuban roots. Maybe that was why my parents wanted me to marry a Cuban man.

No matter who I married, I didn't want those roots to disappear from my life. Perhaps I had not made this clear enough to my parents during the years I had dated Paulo.

Two weeks had passed since our breakup, and I could not get used to the idea of being alone. I kept asking myself, 'Why did I really do it?' That question kept haunting me. Maybe I was tired of hearing my parents asking Paulo when he was planning to go to college and drill him about his past and his brother's involvement with gangs; maybe it was my inability to tell my parents, "This is my life," or perhaps, the pandemic had made me realize the temporary nature of my existence and that I should not settle. Perhaps it was a combination of all these reasons.

It didn't matter to me that Paulo wasn't Cuban or that he didn't attend college, but I couldn't imagine myself without a family. That was a dealbreaker. I knew he didn't want children from the moment we met. I was initially fine with the idea. Then, over the past several months, with so much death happening around me, the thought of my mortality became a reality. Who was going to tell the stories of my grandparents and my father the day I was no longer on this earth?

I had fallen in love with Paulo from the first day I saw him at St. Lawrence Church, after one of his Cuban friends suggested he attend service so he could meet a good Cuban girl. It was love at first sight. When I saw his green eyes and café-con-leche complexion—a mixture of his French and Indian heritages—I didn't have eyes for anyone else. We kept looking at each other and smiling throughout the service. My mother had noticed and touched my hands a couple of times and opened her eyes wide at me. But she could not stop the feelings that had been unleashed within me.

Paulo had grown up in a *favela* (shantytown) on the outskirts of Rio de Janeiro. He never thought he would escape poverty. Then, one day, as he wandered far away from the favela, close to a field where local men played soccer, he discovered a ball hidden in the nearby shrubs. He was eight then. He recalled that day vividly. It was the first ball he had owned, and he felt so happy when he went home with it and showed it to his mother. One of the older kids in the favela began to teach him how to play. Paulo practiced day and night for years until a talent scout discovered him when he was fourteen—three years after his oldest brother died, a victim of gang violence. He decided then he didn't want to bring a child into the world to experience this life.

Paulo moved to Europe after being awarded a contract to play right wing for Lille in France. He scored seventeen goals with seven assists in over one hundred appearances and began to receive more attention from scouts in the United States. Eventually, he found himself in Atlanta after Atlanta United FC purchased his contract.

A sports injury ended Paulo's career when he was twenty-two. Still, with his savings, he moved to Miami, hired a handful of Brazilian and Cuban immigrants, and began a small business that slowly grew. With the money he made, he had been working with an immigration attorney to bring his parents to the United States. What a commendable thing to do!

Yet, now, Paulo was part of my past.

Chapter 2

The Letters

It was a hot, sticky Sunday afternoon—like most summer days tend to be in Tampa, Florida—when I arrived at my grandfather's house two hours earlier than other times, but I didn't bother to call ahead. It was July 11, 2021. After parking my CRV in front of the small beige-color house located on LaSalle Street, I walked toward the porch. I could smell the aroma of freshly cut grass. Purple and yellow flowerbeds adorned either side of the narrow concrete path, and the sounds of heavy traffic from the nearby highway overwhelmed my high-heeled footsteps.

He is so stubborn, I thought, and shook my head as I repositioned the two plastic bags I carried. How many times had I asked him not to mow the lawn? I could pay the boy down the street to do it. But no. He wouldn't allow it.

To avoid scaring him, I knocked on the shiny, dark blue door before retrieving my key from the small purse that hung from the thin strap looping over my shoulder. When I opened the door, I announced, "Grandpa, I'm home. I brought you dinner."

The house had not changed much in twenty years; one wall was full of family pictures, and across from it, pictures of Cuba. The television was off when I walked past the living room on my way to the dining room. It was there where I found him, sitting by the dining room table with letters spread all over it. He looked up at me and adjusted his glasses, "What are you doing here? You scared me!"

"You didn't hear me come in?"

"I must have been distracted. What's in the bags?"

"I brought you dinner from Arco Iris: some ground beef, black beans, and rice, and your favorite dessert."

"Flan?"

"You guessed it."

"Well, just put it on top of the kitchen counter, and I'll put these old letters away."

"Whose are they? Grandma's?"

He shook his head.

"They are just some old letters. I should've thrown them away by now."

"If not grandma's, whose are they? Hers?"

He nodded and inhaled deeply.

"Oh... Can I read them?" I asked, clapping my hands together twice with excitement. He raised his eyebrows and looked up at me.

"Why would you want to read them?"

"No real reason. If they were important enough for you to keep them all these years, I am very interested."

My grandfather waved his hand in a dismissive gesture.

"No. They are going back into this box."

He began to pick them up with his arthritic hands and accommodated a few at a time inside a large shoebox.

"Let me help you," I said and set down the food in an empty section of the table.

"Just take the food to the kitchen."

I ignored him and began to examine one of the letters.

"This one is dated November 15, 1968."

"Yes, it's the first one she sent me. Some of the letters we sent each other are missing, but we managed to save these."

"Over fifty years old," I said in awe. "Please, Grandpa! Let me read them. I will take the box home and return it when I'm done. I promise."

"You're never going to stop asking me, are you? You are just like your mother."

"And she's just like you. I want to know about your past. You are always so secretive, and Mamá doesn't tell me much about your past."

"I haven't shared much with her about my past. She knows I left Cuba with my parents in 1968 when I was twenty-six. I also told her about Cuba before Castro. The rest is best left alone. Anyway, would you like some Cuban coffee? I just made some."

"No, I appreciate it, but if I drink coffee now, I won't be able to sleep."

He shook his head and rolled his eyes. "What kind of Cuban are you?"

"One who loves you very much and wants to know more about you," I said. "So, it's settled. I'll read them. And promise me that if you are ever going to throw them away, you will give them to me. I'll keep them."

He remained silent and allowed me to help him. While we finished putting them away, I said, "I'm surprised you are not watching the news. Things are heating up in Cuba."

"What do you mean?"

"People all over the island are pouring into the streets demanding freedom. They are no longer scared, Grandpa. It's on YouTube."

"YouTube? What's that?"

I giggled. "It's a channel."

He shrugged.

"Let me turn it on for you. You have a smart television and Wi-Fi. That's all you need to get it."

"You're speaking in another language. All I know is that I need to be able to watch my regular channels after you leave."

"I will change it. Mamá said she has never seen anything like it since the triumph of the revolution in 1959. Papá said that people have always been afraid to speak against the government for fear of retribution. Mamá thinks that this is the beginning of a positive change within Cuba."

My grandfather, Rolando, shrugged his shoulders and inhaled deeply.

"Your mom loves to dream. Nothing is going to happen. It has been sixty-two years, and I know I will die without seeing a free Cuba. I have come to accept this."

"Don't be so pessimistic, Grandpa. I also think they are closer than ever before to achieving freedom. When I saw them chanting, there was so much hope in their expressions."

"Think about it," he replied. "Who has the weapons? Who has the power? Who controls it all? The government. That's why nothing will happen."

"I prefer to remain optimistic. Anyhow, let's watch the protests on television, so you see what I mean."

I went to the kitchen to place the food in the refrigerator, then returned to the living room and took the remote control from the coffee table in front of the sofa, where my grandfather was sitting. I sat next to him and searched YouTube for one of the videos I had watched earlier. Moments later, we began to watch the hundreds of people who had flooded the streets, bearing signs that read "freedom," "homeland and life," and chanting.

Conditions within Cuba had not improved after Fidel Castro died in 2016. He had left the country in the hands of his brother Raúl Castro. In April 2021, Raúl stepped down, but he left the island in a severe economic crisis. In 2020, the first year of the pandemic, the economy had contracted by 11%, which increased the scarcity of all necessities.

Once Raúl retired, Miguel Díaz-Canel, who had been the President of Cuba since 2019, consolidated his power over the country, assuming the role of Secretary of the Communist Party.

By July, following the collapse of the healthcare system, people broke the silence. They were no longer scared to go out and protest. However, soon, Díaz-Canel would show the people of Cuba to what extent he would go to maintain power.

As my grandfather and I watched the people, I said, “See what I mean?”

My grandfather smiled bitterly and patted me on the shoulder.

“If you only had experienced a fraction of what Maylin and I had endured, but she stayed in Cuba much longer. She understood what it was like.”

I glanced at him with curiosity. “You have never spoken about her past.”

“I know.”

The central air conditioning unit turned on, and he rubbed his hairy arms with his hands.

We remained silent for a while, watching the people protesting on Havana's streets and in other parts of the island through the feed of homemade YouTube videos. After a while, he began to seem restless.

"Can you just change the channel?" he asked.

"I will, but later, get your tablet. I'm sure your Facebook friends will be sharing more footage from inside the island."

"I belong to a couple of groups. It gives me something to do, so I'll take a look."

I didn't think he would do it. I could tell he was just trying to get me off his back.

"Where is Tía Rita?" I asked, changing the channel to where my grandfather had it when I first turned on the television. I then shut it off.

"She went to the store. I'm glad. I needed some peace."

"You know you love your sister."

"She can't stay quiet for one moment! I need tranquility. Then, she gets mad when I tell her to stop telling me stories about her friends. You want to hear the latest?"

"What did she do now?"

"She wants me to go out with one of her friends! She knows it hasn't been a year yet since my wife died. Besides, who would want to go out with someone like me, old and grumpy?"

"Don't say that, Grandpa! Any woman would be lucky to go out with such a handsome gentleman. Look at you! You still have a full set of hair, your face is always shaven, and your mustache is perfectly trimmed. And when you wear those Cuban guayabera shirts, ladies, watch out!"

"Now you are laughing at me."

"I would never do that, my gordito."

"Now you are calling me fat!"

"Not true. I used the diminutive form. Men look more interesting when they have a little meat on their bones."

"No more talking about me. So, when are you getting married? You are twenty-four already."

"I don't have a boyfriend, Grandpa. Remember? I broke up with Paulo. Besides, I'm in no hurry."

"What are you waiting for? For me to die before you decide to give me great-grandchildren?"

"It's only been a couple of weeks since we broke up. Besides, it's hard to date in the middle of the pandemic."

"You're probably right. At least you're vaccinated now, so it's a little safer to be out and about."

"Yes, but there are a lot of breakthrough infections out there. I'm a little afraid because I don't want to bring this virus home to you."

"I can't wait for this pandemic to be over so life can go back to normal."

I inhaled. "I agree. Well, I'll be heading out now. Tell Tía Rita I stopped by. Give her some flan. You have to watch your sugar."

"I'll think about it."

I kissed my grandfather on the cheek, grabbed the box of letters, and left.

Chapter 3

November 15, 1968

My summer vacation was about to begin, and I had not read the letters. I wanted to find the appropriate time and place, and the beach sounded like the perfect spot. Any other year, I would have traveled to Miami or another state, but with the COVID-19 pandemic in full swing, I decided to stay close to home.

My parents were vacationing in St. Augustine, so my best friend Maggie and I rented a room at Opal's Sand Resort in Clearwater Beach, which had a balcony overlooking the popular sandy shore.

Maggie and I had met at the University of South Florida in the Managerial Accounting class. She was a good listener, but she was always critical of her appearance. I kept telling her there was nothing wrong with being a few pounds over the ideal weight.

"You say that because you're thin," she would tell me. I could not convince her to stop worrying about how others perceived her.

Before we went on vacation, she came to visit me one night.

November 15, 1968

"I can't wait for you to read those letters and tell me all about them!" she said when I told her about the box. "To be able to experience a unique moment in time, one that will never repeat, is so exciting!"

Her grin exposed her teeth. I, too, was anxious to read them, and yet, I felt like an intruder.

As I prepared for my vacation, I organized the letters by date, all along with thinking about the secrets I would uncover. I noticed a gap of several years in the dates. Perhaps my grandfather had the missing letters at home. I decided to read them up to the last date before the gap.

My cousin Marta called while I was sorting the letters. My mother told her about my vacation, and she asked if she could visit me for a couple of days.

"I'm sorry," I said. "If I had paid for the place myself, I would have invited you, but my friend paid for the entire stay."

I had to lie. My mother had always taught me that family was everything, and I felt guilty about lying. I just needed time to gather my thoughts after my breakup.

Maggie and I checked into the hotel around 2 p.m. After unpacking, she stayed inside the room, studying for the Certified Public Accounting examination. I went outside to the balcony with the box of letters and a glass of Pinot Grigio. I placed the glass on a small table next to my chair, opened the box, and retrieved the oldest one. All of them had turned yellow over time, but the cursive blue-ink writing on this one, neat and legible, was easy to read, so different from the often-cryptic scribbles that sometimes, not even *I* could decipher. I closed the box, leaned back, and began to read while the ocean air inundated my senses:

Dear Rolando,

I am so excited! According to Mamá's estimates, we should be in the United States by Christmas. I can't wait to be there with you!

She told me that two flights are going from Miami to the beach town of Varadero (Cuba) twice a day, which is a lot less dangerous than leaving through the Port of Camarioca.

I was eighteen in 1965 when the Camarioca Boatlift was taking place. You remember that exodus. But Mamá said back then it was unsafe to leave by boat, so we waited. In some ways, I was glad because we got to meet that year at Maritza's house on her eighteenth birthday celebration. I couldn't believe that living in the same neighborhood, only a few blocks away, I had never noticed you.

I don't know why Mamá thinks that an airplane is less dangerous than a boat. I'm a little scared to fly.

I am glad we are leaving, but my brother Raul won't be able to join us. He's of military age and has to enlist in the service. It may be a few years before he's able to leave. You know how that works because you, too, had to wait. My parents wanted to stay because of him, but my aunt convinced them to go. She will take care of my brother. She, too, has a son of military age, her only son.

I miss you.

Every corner of Zapote Street reminds me of you, from the narrow hallway between your house and the apartment building next door where we used to kiss when no one was watching to the Santos Suárez Park, where we sat on a bench to hold hands and watch the orange flamboyant trees in full bloom.

Your house is not empty anymore. I don't like passing by and watching strangers sitting on the front porch. Revolutionaries live there, I hear, a couple and their two sons, a ten and a twelve-year-old. They don't pay much attention to those children. I often see them on the street corner crushing almonds that fall from a tree, shirtless, even now when the heat of the summer is gone and cooler days have returned.

I wanted to tell you more, but I promised my mother I would clean the house. I try to help her as much as I can. When you write, tell me about Miami. I can't wait to see you. I dream about you, about us, all the time.

I will see you soon, my love.

Hugs and kisses,

Maylin

Chapter 4

January 15, 1969

Dear Maylin,

I just received the letter you sent me back in November. The mail is taking so long. I was hoping you would be here by now, but I heard from my parents that at the last minute, your parents decided to stay because they could not get themselves to leave your brother behind. I understand their position, but what about us?

I think about you all the time, especially when I see a couple walking by and holding hands. Know that I'm willing to wait as long as necessary. I am that committed to you, to that bright smile and dark eyes that keep me up at night.

You wanted me to tell you about Miami. I stay busy. Time goes by faster that way.

I am attending college in the evenings and working at my uncle's furniture business during the day. If I save enough money, one day, I will be able to buy my own place, a place for the two of us.

Life here is so different from that in Cuba, even though my family tries to surround themselves with Cubans like us so they feel more at home.

I am trying to get used to a new language and a different way of life. I see a lot of hippies on television and at school. The ladies are not shy like they were in Cuba. But you have nothing to worry about.

And talking about a different subject, you know how much I like American music. Well, from December 28 to December 30, the Gulfstream Park, right outside Miami, hosted the Miami Pop Festival. Over 100,000 people came! Some of my friends from college went and said how much they liked it.

Can you imagine?

The Grateful Dead, Chuck Berry, and Marvin Gaye? I wish I could have been there, but there are more important things I need to do, like saving money for us, for that little family we will have one day.

I already picture it: two girls with long black hair and fair skin like you, and a boy who is into music and sports like me. The perfect family. That's my dream.

As you know, my parents had two children, but my oldest brother died of diphtheria when I was five. My parents were never the same, making me feel sometimes as if when I lost my brother, I also lost part of my parents. My mother would spend hours looking at pictures of my brother and crying, and my father retreated into his head. He looked numb.

Feeling so alone made me strong. At the same time, it made me wish I had a big family. Hopefully, you can make this dream come true one day.

Keep writing to me, and don't give up on us. We will be together again soon.

Until next time, my beautiful doll.

January 15, 1969

Love always,

Rolando

Lena took a deep breath after reading this letter and became pensive. *Grandpa is into rock music?* she thought. She glanced at her iPhone. As she was reading the letter, a text message had arrived from her Paulo.

"We need to talk," he said.

She thought about responding. Instead, she shut down her phone and took another sip of wine. She was ready for the next letter.

Chapter 5

September 15, 1969

Dear Maylin,

I sent you three letters, and I have not received any responses. In the last two, I didn't have much to say. I'm still saving money. I need to live with my parents for now to help them financially so they can stop renting and save money to buy a nice place for the two of us.

My uncle told me that in the United States if you want to get ahead, you have to buy your own place. Otherwise, it's like throwing money in the garbage. It makes sense to me.

Of course, you can plan as much as you want, and sometimes, life changes those plans. So, here is what happened. I took a break from college to save money faster, and I was drafted. So many of my friends are against the Vietnam War, but what kind of person would I be if I burned my draft card like many of them are doing?

I have read about what's going on. Back in 1965, President Lyndon Johnson said that he had no choice but to send men into battle because North Vietnam and communist China wanted to take over

South Vietnam. That's the last thing the United States and the world need.

You know all too well what communism can do to a country, and I will be careful here. I don't want you to get in trouble, and I know some letters from the United States are read in Cuba before they reach their destination. I feel that it is my obligation to go. Mamá is very scared for my safety. She is praying a lot to Our Lady of Charity these days. I tell her not to worry.

Right now, there is no end in sight to this war. Hopefully, by the time it ends, you will be here. Please keep sending me letters. I will need them more than ever now. Send them to my mother, and she will find a way to get them to me.

I love you very much.

Many hugs and kisses.

Rolando

Chapter 6

January 4, 1970

Dear Rolando,

When I received your letter in which you told me you were going to Vietnam, I was frightened. I cannot imagine you being on the other side of the world in a confrontation that has nothing to do with you, but I understand your sense of duty to your new country.

You will probably be in Vietnam by the time this letter arrives. Please be careful. Think of that family you want to have with me one day and stay safe for all of us.

About Cuba, many of our neighbors, girls I grew up with, have left, and new people are moving in, even a Russian woman who is married to a Cuban man. I don't know why anyone would ever want to move here. Life is not like it used to be. The rations we can buy at the grocery store of rice, beans, meats, and other basic foods keep getting smaller. Sometimes, beef doesn't come at all. Sometimes, for breakfast, I have water sweetened with sugar and a piece of bread. Mami also makes a lot of potaje de chícharos (split pea soup). I am sick of it, but for some reason, chícharos are not in short supply.

January 4, 1970

Regarding the reasons why I have not written, I have been a little down with so much going on.

In September, at the start of the school year, my younger sister, Elisa, was taken to work in the fields. She is only thirteen, and Mamá was very worried about her being away from home for several weeks. She says that girls that age should not be working like farmers, pulling weeds from tomato farms and picking okra and coffee beans.

She says that girls should be allowed to have a childhood. God knows life is difficult enough. Mamá prayed for her every day. To take food to my sister, she would buy cans of condensed milk in the black market and place them in the pressure cooker for about 40 minutes. The milk turned into a thick, caramel-looking custard that tasted delicious.

Mamá had to take several buses to travel to the camp where my sister was held, out there in the middle of nowhere. But, per the camp rules, she could only visit her on weekends. I went with her a few times. My sister practically lived off the milk we brought her because the rice that she was served at the camp had weevils in it, and she refused to eat it.

My sister doesn't want to return to the camps next year. She said it was so cold in the morning when she and the other girls were taken to the fields in the back of a truck before sunrise that she caught a bad cold. However, she was not allowed to come home. She said there was also no privacy in the bathrooms, and the food was inedible. I don't know what Mamá is going to do. She won't have a choice but to send her. The government requires it.

I don't think I have told you that I started attending the University of Havana. Mamá wants me to keep educating myself in case we are able to leave. Not that an education is going to do me much good in Cuba. Mamá has friends who are college graduates who are working as taxi drivers.

There are no horror stories I could tell you that would compare to what you must be experiencing, I'm sure. Instead, I will leave you with this memory of us during our last vacation together, walking on the sands of Varadero Beach, holding hands while the sun began to hide over the horizon. Remember how Mamá, standing on the sand, kept asking us to come home for dinner?

I have always wondered how we were able to go to the beach when you were here last summer. She later told me that one of her revolutionary friends had been awarded a vacation on the beach and had invited us to come for two days.

My love, come back alive. When things get rough, think of us, of the happy times. I will always keep you in my heart.

Kisses,

Maylin

Chapter 7

March 15, 1970

Dear Rolando,

I have not received a letter from you since I last wrote, but I'm not surprised. Who knows what you are going through?

I don't have much to say. Cuba has stayed inside a time capsule. I am learning at the university that the Soviet Union is heavily subsidizing us. It makes me wonder how life would be here if it weren't that way.

We try to do the best we can. We go to the Sorrento Pizzeria in the Santos Suárez neighborhood once every other month. I'm sure you remember the pizza they made there. It's so good. However, we cannot afford to go there often.

Sometimes, Mamá gives me some money so that my sister and I can go to the movie theater and other times; we visit El Coppélia in El Vedado for a scoop of ice cream. It's a very popular place, but the lines can be long, especially on weekends.

My brother is still fulfilling his military service and comes home when we least expect it. He has been more quiet than usual these days. It's like he is hiding something. Mamá is always thinking the worst. She worries about him so much. I think that is why she refuses to leave without him. Somehow, she thinks she can protect him when she's here.

I don't have much more to say. I anxiously await to hear from you.

Love,

Maylin

Chapter 8

June 15, 1970

Dear Maylin,

I received your January 4th letter and placed it inside a little plastic bag for safekeeping. I carry it with me all the time. It gives me hope.

I don't want to worry you with the horrible details of war. The things I have witnessed, the death, the destruction, the hatred, and the love that somehow manage to coexist under the most inhumane of conditions...

I can see why so many men are against the war, but I can't think that way if I'm going to get out of here alive. And I must stay alive for you.

The men in my platoon are from eight different states, some drafted and some enlisted, but I'm the only Cuban. My best friend, Tom, is from Alabama. He is a black guy, much bigger and stronger than me, who has saved my life a couple of times. I will always be indebted to him and his family. I didn't know that people from Alabama ate fried pork skin, like Cubans do. He also likes fried fish and grits. I haven't tried that combination.

Then, there is a Jerry from New Orleans who is always talking about life in the bayou. In Bayou Country, most homes can be reached by boat. These are swampy areas where the Creole and

Cajun cultures prevail. For him, the military is a way out of the bayou. He told me about foods I had never tried, like gumbo, jambalaya, and crawfish.

Jerry fell in love with a Vietnamese girl. He wants to marry her and bring her to America. I, on the other hand, can only think about the beautiful girl I left on Zapote Street.

You know what would be nice? I want to take you with me to Louisiana and Alabama when I return from the war. We could visit my friends and taste all the great food in those areas. It makes my mouth water to think of them, but most of all, I miss having a nice cup of café con leche with a piece of buttered toast in the mornings.

Well, I have to run. I just heard my name called. Until next time, my doll.

Yours always,

Rolando

Chapter 9

November 14, 1970

Dear Maylin,

I don't know when you will receive this letter. I didn't want to write until my condition improved, but at last, I'm going home.

In July, I was part of a confrontation between the U.S. Army 101st Airborne Division and the People's Army of Vietnam at the Fire Support Base Ripcord in the A-Shu Valley in South Vietnam. The heaviest fighting took place in the first 23 days of July when 75 of our men were killed. Ultimately, the U.S. command ordered the evacuation of the base. The night of July 9th was quiet, but Brigade Intelligence was anticipating an NVA (North Vietnamese Army) attack, so we were all very tense. The winds were strong throughout the day, and that evening, a strange, ominous feeling came over me. I came to think that I would die that night. However, we were not assaulted that evening.

On July 10, I was so scared, still anticipating the worst. But when the artillery attack started, and we hunkered down, the adrenaline and the training we had received kicked in. It was kill or be killed. After enduring heavy fire for a while, I was severely wounded by mortar rounds. There was so much blood that I had to be evacuated and sent to a hospital.

As bad as that sounds, I was one of the lucky ones. Jerry, my friend from New Orleans, didn't make it. A mortar round killed him on the spot. And to make things worse, his Vietnamese girlfriend is pregnant with his child. Just a couple of days before his death, he was telling me how excited he was about the idea of being a father. He was afraid something was going to happen to him. Many of us were.

"If something happens to me, give my girlfriend my U.S. Army dog tag so she can pass it on to my son or daughter," he said. When I was in the hospital, I heard that his wishes were fulfilled. Part of me wonders about the future of that child. For the Vietnamese, his father will always be an enemy.

On the same day Jerry was killed, another one of our troops was killed, and three were wounded when they tripped a trap in a minefield during a reconnaissance mission.

I still have nightmares and wake up in the middle of the night, sweating and screaming, thinking about all the men we lost. I have these strange flashbacks. It's like I'm reliving the worst moments in Vietnam all over again. Sometimes, there are obvious causes, such as a loud noise. Other times, they just happen.

I keep thinking, why did I survive, and they had to die? It is something that will haunt me for the rest of my life.

November 14, 1970

I am sorry that this letter was not like the hopeful and cheerful ones you have received from me in the past. War changes men. It changed me, but it has not changed how I feel about you. I still dream of the day when we will be together again.

During my long recovery period at a hospital, away from everyone I loved, I sometimes told myself to stop trying to get better. Then I read your letters, the ones I kept inside a plastic bag that luckily didn't get destroyed when I was shot.

Only the thought of going back to you kept me alive. Hopefully, that dream is closer to becoming a reality.

Love,

Rolando

Chapter 10

December 15, 1970

Dear Rolando,

For several days, I debated with myself. Should I tell you the news? God knows you have enough to deal with. But I didn't want you to find out from someone else. I sent you a couple of letters telling you what happened. The fact that your July letter doesn't mention it tells me you never received them. I was so upset when I wrote them that they probably never left Cuba. I told you that the rumor here is that our mail is sometimes read. My letters probably had too many truths about what was going on.

So, once again, this is what happened.

My love, in May, the Cuban government stopped allowing people to leave. The Freedom Flights continue for those who have already been waiting for their turn to leave, but that's all. I hear we have lost too much professional talent to exile, but who knows? How can they just hold people here just like that?

I hope you understand what that means for us. I won't be able to leave Cuba. After screaming, crying, and falling into depression for several days, acceptance began to rear its head.

December 15, 1970

Resignation. That's all those who stayed on this Godforsaken island have left.

I want you to fight to stay alive and return home from that awful war in Viet Nam. I want you to meet someone, have that beautiful family you've always dreamed of, and visit your friends in all those wonderful cities you've always wanted to see. Enjoy life for the two of us, you hear me?

Our dream was not meant to be, but the memories of us walking in Santos Suarez Park, holding hands, when we thought no one could ever tear us apart, will remain with me forever.

I will always love you,

Maylin

Chapter 11

March 12, 1971

Dear Rolando,

When I read your November 14 letter, in which you told me that you were badly wounded and hospitalized, I could hardly breathe. My mother came into the room after I managed to burst into tears, and when she learned what was going on, she rushed to the kitchen to get me some linden tea. I am so sorry about everything.

By now, you should have read my December correspondence.

I wish our story would have had a different ending. I love you so much; it physically hurts me that we can't be together.

Mamá keeps telling me that everyone is born with a predetermined destiny. "There is nothing you can do against your destiny," she tells me. You have no idea how angry I get when she says that. Now, I wonder if she's right.

I have considered leaving the university, but then what would I do? Get a government job, the only type of job any of us can do, and do that for the rest of my life? So, I'll finish my degree to at least feel a sense of accomplishment.

March 12, 1971

Almost two years have passed since you left, and my parents think it's time for me to start dating again. There is a guy at the university who has been after me for the last three months. He seems nice and is studying engineering. Sometimes, he picks up flowers from the park and brings them to me, but I'm not ready.

About Cuba, not much is happening. We still need ration cards to buy our food. Sometimes, the water shuts down, and trucks come to deliver it. We go outside with buckets and stand in line until it is our turn to fill them. Other times, the electricity goes off for hours, especially at night. It happens frequently, but we have a Chinese kerosene lamp that we place on the dining room table to finish any remaining house chores.

After we're done, we turn it off and go to the porch, just like the other neighbors. We talked for a little while, and then my parents rocked themselves in our old rocking chairs until they fell asleep. I stay there, quiet, listening to the neighbors. Yes, I know what you're thinking. I have become nosy. You're right. It gives me something to do.

In summer months, in particular, it becomes unbearable to stay inside without the ability to turn on a fan. But whether it's winter or summer, we sleep with our windows open. Then, flying roaches come into the house, and I am terrified of them.

I know what you must be thinking. None of these stories compares to what you have lived through. Hopefully, by the time you receive this letter, you will be enjoying all the comforts of home, just like you did before you left.

A big and warm embrace. Please write to me when you can, even after you find that lucky girl who will occupy my place. Your letters will be my only window to that world that has been taken away from me. I will always love you, but love is learning to let go.

That's why I am letting you go.

Now that you have learned about death and destruction, value your life and live it to its maximum potential.

I wish you a life full of joy.

Hugs,

Maylin

Chapter 12

May 25, 1971

Dear Maylin,

I read your letters. My mother had kept them for me until my arrival.

I wasn't expecting to read what you wrote. I kept reading your last letter, hoping I had misread it. I then threw it on the bed and stormed out of my room. My mother asked me where I was going, but I didn't answer. I needed to get away from everyone, so I started to drive without knowing where I was going. After a while, I ended up on the highway, on I-95. I drove as fast as I could, and you have no idea all the crazy things that came to mind. I kept seeing you saying goodbye at Rancho Boyeros Airport in Havana. I saw my dead friend, and even saw myself back in Vietnam.

My mother thinks I should get counseling, but I am a man. I had to resolve my problems the way men did, so I started going to a gym. I drown my anger by hitting a punching bag over and over again until my heart feels as if it is going to pop out of my chest. The other day, I started hitting the bag without gloves to feel the pain of the punches, but the trainer insisted I put the gloves back on. He didn't want me to cause damage to my knuckles like I care.

May 25, 1971

After my honorable discharge, I stayed at home for a couple of weeks. However, the days felt long. I needed to feel useful, so I went back to work. In August, I will return to university. Staying busy should help. That's what my mother keeps telling me.

My friend Tom was wounded on the same day as me and is already home. I told you about him. He was the one who saved me a couple of times. He's from Alabama. Perhaps when I finish classes, I will visit him.

I know you want me to move on. I don't know how. Not yet. A couple of my American friends invited me to go to a bar with them. Maybe I'll go.

Well, I'm not sure how to close this letter. What should I say? Until we see each other again?

No matter what happens, no one can take away the moments we shared. Those belong to us and will unite us forever.

Love,

Rolando

Chapter 13

September 15, 1971

Dear Rolando,

It has been a year and four months since the government stopped allowing people to leave, and over two years since you left.

Things are so different now than when you and I were growing up.

My grandfather owned a store before 1959, and my grandmother stayed home. My brother and I loved spending time with her. She always had a delicious treat waiting for us, either guava marmalade with cheese or chunks of fruta bomba (papaya) in a heavy syrup, all homemade.

Today, several years after the government confiscated their business, she cries when I go to her house, as she has nothing to offer me. "Abuela, don't worry," I tell her. But she misses that old Cuba when she didn't need a ration card to buy what she needed.

Sometimes, she buys guava marmalade from a neighbor who has connections and is able to purchase the ingredients on the black market. Still, we must spend more and more of the little money we have on the necessities of life, with little left for luxuries like guava marmalade.

September 15, 1971

For special occasions, such as birthdays—or recently, when my brother finished his military service—my mother makes her mayonnaise at home. She uses it for her macaroni salad to serve at small family gatherings, accompanied by cake and lemonade. It might sound gross, but I enjoy mixing the macaroni salad with the cake. There's something about that combination of sweet and salty that I find appealing.

And changing the theme, my brother worries me. He doesn't act like the same person he used to be before enlisting in the military. He is quiet and doesn't engage much in conversations around the table. Luckily, his girlfriend comes over on weekends, and they take a bus to Santa Maria Beach. He returns late at night looking more cheerful, like before. My mother thinks he needs time. I believe he's angry that we are stuck here because of him. I spoke with him the other night and shared my thoughts. He remained silent and looked down. "It's not your fault," I said. "There is only one individual responsible for what is happening. We all know who that is."

He lifted his head and glanced at me for a moment. Then, he walked out of the room.

Rolando, there's something I've been wanting to tell you. My parents have been insisting I move on. They said I needed to make the best of our situation. At first, I held onto the idea that something would change, that there was a chance the government would reverse its position. Then, I lost hope.

September 15, 1971

Recently, I met someone at the university. He chased me for a while, but quite frankly, I wasn't in the mood to date anyone. He then asked one of my friends for my address and showed up at my house with some guavas and a pound of sugar for my mother. That's all it took for her to like him.

My mother tells me I should give Carlos a chance. I am thinking about it. In the meantime, I hope that you have met someone who makes you happy. Life must go on, and no matter what crumbles around us, we must make the best of the short time we are here on earth. My grandmother tells me that all the time.

A big hug to you.

Maylin

Chapter 14

Vacation

I had read the last letter from Cuba before the gap. The next one, from Maylin, was dated April 26, 1980. What had happened in between?

When I went back inside our hotel room with the box of letters, I found Maggie immersed in her studies.

"Already done?" she asked me, shifting her attention from her CPA review material on her laptop.

"No. I don't want to read the others without knowing what happened during the years in which they didn't exchange letters."

"Are you calling your grandfather to ask him?"

"It's best if I wait until I see him again."

"You have to tell me all about it later! And before I forget, our mutual friend Mark called. He heard we were here together and would like to meet with us for dinner later. He'll bring one of his friends. He said he tried to call you, but your phone is off."

"Yes, Paulo sent me a message. I didn't want to hear from him or anyone else."

"Are you going to respond to Paulo?"

I looked away and placed the letters on top of a cabinet.

"I need a new start. He's part of my past."

Maggie glanced at me.

"Why are you looking at me like that?"

"How?"

"Never mind."

"Well, can we go out tonight?"

"I have nothing better to do," I said.

"Great! I'll call Mark and tell him."

"Where are we going?"

"Palm Pavilion Grill. It's right on the beach with romantic sunsets and all."

"I'm not ready to start dating anyone, so don't get any ideas."

"Whatever you say."

"And how did Mark know my number? We haven't talked in years. Why would he call me?"

Maggie shrugged. "I'm sure he found out about your breakup."

"But you didn't tell him anything, right?"

"Me? I'm totally innocent. All I have been doing is studying for the CPA exam. I need to pass it the first time because that will open a lot of doors. So don't blame me."

I looked at her, trying to ascertain whether she was telling me the truth. She didn't appear to be lying. She didn't play with her fingers or move nervously in her seat.

"Well, I'm going for a swim. Need to cool down," I said. "You want to come?"

"Sure," she replied, closing her laptop. "I can use a break. It will be the perfect time to hear about the letters."

After changing into our swimsuits, me a two-piece red bikini and she a black one-piece, we went outside and walked toward the beach. Life went on around me: laughter, children at play, and sunbathers. I could hear music playing in the distance and people speaking in different languages. I recognized those I was familiar with: Spanish, English, and Italian.

The heat emanated from the white sand, enticing me to get in the water faster. I left my towel on the sand and sprinted toward the beach while I felt the sun's rays burning my skin. It was then I remembered I had forgotten the sunblock in the room, which would guarantee that I would look like a lobster if I stayed at the beach too long.

"You want to leave our stuff here?" I heard Maggie say.

"Yes," I shouted without looking back. "Let's go."

The moment my feet touched the water, I felt its warmth, inviting me to go deeper. The sand beneath felt soft. I thought about my grandfather. He told me that as pretty as Clearwater Beach was, no beach in the world could compare to the beaches in Cuba.

"Yes, Grandpa. Everything in Cuba was better."

"Before Castro," he would clarify.

I giggled when I thought about my grandfather. Then, I took a few more steps until the water reached my middle torso. Not far from us, I noticed a couple locked in an embrace, which brought me memories of the last time Paulo and I had been there. I felt a little jealous.

"The water feels so good," said Maggie, splashing her hands in it like a child.

"The temperature is perfect."

The calmness of the waters and the beauty of the buildings lining up the coast, as far as my eyes could see, relaxed me. It's no wonder this beach is so popular with many European tourists.

We swam for a while and talked about the letters, Paulo, my over-protective parents, and Maggie's understanding family, who had trusted her to make the right decisions. She, too, had broken up with her boyfriend. Actually, he left her because he claimed she didn't devote enough time to him. I couldn't tolerate someone that needy. That was one of the things I liked about Paulo. He was understanding, and we had given each other our space.

The idea of starting over scared me. Life was complicated enough without getting to know someone new, but as Maggie said, it could always be worse.

I thought about Marta and wondered if she had called Paulo.

"Marta wanted to join us," I said.

"Here?"

"Yes, but I told her you had paid for the place and didn't want visitors."

Maggie opened her blue eyes wide. "Why are you making me look like the bad one?"

"I know. I feel bad. Maybe I should call her. She's family."

"She was trying to steal your boyfriend. You don't have to feel bad about not inviting her, only about blaming me."

"Sorry about that. I do feel bad. She can't afford to stay at a place like this."

"Worry about yourself for a change. If you still feel guilty by tomorrow, maybe you can ask her to stay here Friday night."

"That's a good idea."

"I just realized something," Maggie said, interlacing her fingers.

"What?"

"In comparison to you and most Cubans I know, I live a very boring life. Nothing exciting ever happens in my life."

"You must be referring to my father and my grandfather."

"I'm referring to your cousin Marta and all the drama your mom makes because Paulo is not Cuban. And yes, your father and grandfather also have lived eventful lives."

"The Irish are not that different than the Cubans. You have a very rich and troublesome history."

"True, but it doesn't dominate every aspect of our lives."

"You're probably right. It's almost as if someone who has lived in Cuba never truly leaves Cuba behind. It is as if..."

"They are possessed by the island!"

"Now you're making fun of me. I will not say anything else to you if you keep going."

We laughed. We stayed in the water for a couple of hours until Maggie told me that my face and shoulders had started to turn red.

Later, before sundown, Maggie and I found ourselves inside Mark's convertible BMW.

"Have you been to the Palm Pavilion before?" Mark asked us while lowering his sunglasses and exposing his brown eyes to look at me through the rearview mirror. I could smell his musky cologne from where I was sitting.

"I don't think I have," I said, still wondering how Mark knew to call me.

"You ladies look hot tonight," he added.

"I look like a hot mess," said Maggie.

I shook my head. "Stop saying that. You look lovely in that strapless dress. Doesn't she, Mark?"

Mark looked back for a brief moment and then refocused on the road. "Beautiful!" he said.

"It has been so long since the last time you and I talked, Mark," I said. "How did you know I was here?"

Mark and I had been in the same circles while growing up, not only because he had danced with me during my Quince. We kept seeing each other at parties, such as the annual Tampa Hispanic Heritage Man and Woman of the Year celebrations, the last one held in 2019, just a few months before the pandemic.

However, my parents did not achieve the same level of success as he did. His father was a doctor, and his mother was a pharmacist. My mother worked at Tampa General Hospital as a human resources generalist, and my father was an electrical engineer.

"I was told not to say," he replied.

"Mamá put you up to this," I concluded.

Mark laughed. "You know her well," he said. "She talked to my mother and told her about Paulo and the three qualities she wanted, which I happen to meet, by the way."

Tom, Mark's friend, shook his head.

"I've seen the type of girls you go after," I said. "I don't fit the mold."

"Are you calling me superficial?"

"If the shoe fits."

"That hurt!"

"Sorry. It wasn't my intention. I'm just angry about what my mother did," I said. "If I had known this, I would've never accepted going out with you! I'm not a charity case."

"Listen, Lena. It's not a big deal. It's a meal. Let's just enjoy ourselves. After losing my oldest sister to this new Delta variant, I know we can't take life for granted."

"Your sister passed away? Oh no! I am so sorry. When?"

"Two weeks ago. She had various health issues and wasn't vaccinated, even though my father had begged her to do it. My father was devastated. If she had sought medical care sooner, he was confident he could have saved her, but she waited. She didn't want him to tell her, 'I told you so.'"

"My mother didn't tell me anything."

"My parents kept her death to themselves. It's still too soon, and they have not come to terms with her loss. They think they've failed her."

"She was a grown woman. There is nothing they could have done. I'm truly sorry."

"I'm sorry, man," Tom, Mark's friend, who sat in the front next to him, said. Maggie echoed his words.

"Well, no more talk about this," Mark said. "Let's have a good time. All the food and drinks are on me."

"I'm not going to allow you to do that. Either we go Dutch or else."

Mark removed his sunglasses and once again looked at me through the rearview mirror. "Lena, let me do this," he said with sadness in his eyes. I didn't say anything.

We had a nice dinner accompanied by lively conversation, but I kept noticing that, at times, Mark's mind would travel far away. When we were done, Maggie wanted to explore the shops along the beach. I was in no mood for shops and decided to walk on the sand. Mark joined me.

"I'm sorry again about your sister," I said.

"Me too, and I'm sorry that you and your boyfriend broke up."

Mark and I walked along the beach for a while, talking about our times at the university and in high school. We had taken some business classes together and had collaborated on some projects during our college years. Our mothers were friends and wanted us to start dating. Once, I heard my mother telling him when she visited how she wished I would leave the "Brazilian."

Mark would have been a good catch for any woman: tall, handsome, educated, and approachable. Part of me thought he was too good-looking for my taste. He was the type of guy who knew women would always look in his direction when he entered a room, a man who acted with all the assurance in the world. Guys like him couldn't avoid acting obnoxious at times like they were God's gift to women. No, thank you. I was too insecure about myself to have a man of his looks in my life.

On this night, Mark seemed more vulnerable than at other times. He listened attentively and asked me many questions, as if he genuinely cared about my life. So, I shared more personal things with him than I would have been inclined to do any other time. I told him about my grandfather's letters, the reasons why I had broken up with Paulo, and my lack of plans for the future. I couldn't look past the following week, no matter how hard I tried. He empathized.

"You will figure out what to do. You're a smart young woman."

"Maybe you're right," I said.

Yet, no matter what anyone said, I could not help feeling like a ship without a rudder.

Chapter 15

The Gap

I went to my grandfather's house on Saturday, after my vacation ended, anxious to know what had happened during the nine years in which no letters had been exchanged between him and Maylin. I knocked as usual before using my key, but this time, the friendly and smiley face of Tía Rita greeted me. I hugged her and kissed her on the cheek.

"You want some Cuban coffee?" she asked. "I can make you some."

"No, don't worry. I'm hyper enough."

"Nonsense. Cuban coffee gives us our passion. Look at everything we have accomplished in this country. You know how?"

"Yes, I know. It's the coffee!"

We both laughed and went inside. Tía Rita sat in a rocking chair, and I sat on the sofa. She dressed in a colorful flower-print blouse with two-thirds sleeves, white pants, and sandals that made her appear younger than her age, especially with her well-manicured nails and bracelets around her wrist.

"So, how was your vacation?" she asked, glancing at me with eyes wide open and a smile.

"I enjoyed myself," I said. A half-truth.

She said she couldn't believe how I could enjoy myself without my boyfriend by my side.

"Tía Rita, you know why we broke up. I don't want to talk about him."

"He called and asked me about you," she replied. "He has something important to tell you, but you know him. I asked him if I could give you the message, and he insisted on telling you himself."

I changed the subject and asked her about my grandfather.

"A friend of his picked him up to take him to Arco Iris."

"A male friend?" I asked.

"No, female, from when we lived in Cuba. She asked him out as a friend. They were both lonely and met through Facebook recently after she moved to Tampa. They met through the All Things Cuban group."

"I'm a member, too. I have learned a lot about Cuba through the members in that group."

"Have you been keeping up with the situation in Cuba?"

I shook my head. I had not paid attention to Cuba during my vacation. It stressed me out to see the repression that followed the protests of July 11th. Hundreds had been taken out of their houses, beaten, and jailed. The hospitals had collapsed due to the number of COVID-19 cases. I could not see all that tragedy happening in front of my eyes as people from Cuba shared home videos on social media.

"Well, in August, just a couple of days ago, many videos from inside the island stopped coming after the Cuban government passed a resolution restricting freedom of expression on social media under Decreto-Ley 35. People are now obligated to stop the diffusion of 'false news.' It also prohibits the use of the internet in ways that impact the 'security of the collective,' 'general well-being,' and 'public morality.' People understood by those measures that if they said anything negative about the government, they could be jailed."

"It's awful what is happening," I said.

"Many people around the world are supporting the protestors. Here in Tampa, I have attended a few protests myself, but it's so hot outside. I don't know how people can stand out there for so long in this humid and unbearable heat. A woman almost passed out from exhaustion."

"You must be careful, especially with this new Delta variant being more contagious than previous ones," I said.

Tía Rita had experienced the wrath of the pandemic at the very beginning when her husband died a couple of weeks after contracting COVID-19. She, too, became infected but somehow managed to recover. She couldn't stay in her house alone after that. Her two adult children then encouraged her to sell her house and move in with her brother.

After a while, I switched topics and shared with her the real purpose of my visit.

"I have been reading the letters Grandpa kept," I said. "But there is a gap."

"I can't believe he allowed you to take them. He was so mad at me when he returned from a store one day and found me reading them. I still managed to get my way. He argues and gets angry, but in the end, he is a gentle and kind old man."

"So, what happened?"

"It's too bad those two were split up," she said, adjusting her glasses. "So much time lost."

"What happened during that time?"

"Life happened."

"What do you mean?"

"He married your grandmother. Maylin married Carlos, the guy she met at the university."

My thin and petite grandaunt, who measured no more than five feet, leaned back and crossed her legs. She did not appear to be a woman in her mid-sixties.

"Did he love Grandma?"

She remained silent for a moment, uncrossed her legs, and moved forward in her chair.

"Look. You are probably too young to understand these things, but love is a fluid concept. He loved your grandmother in a very different way than his first love. Your grandmother came into his life during a time when your grandfather was a broken man. She was the right person to take him out of the hole he was in."

"How did they meet?"

"Matilda, your grandmother, was a nurse, first at MacDill's airbase and then, as you know, at the veterans' hospital. I'm so glad they found each other. My grandmother used to say that God doesn't always give us what we want, but what we need. In his case, I think it's true."

"Was he happy with her?"

"Matilda was a very caring woman. She did things for him I would not have done. Well, you'll see when you read the other letters. He was blessed to have found her."

"Was my grandfather upset that Maylin was the first one to suggest they move on and meet other people?"

"He hasn't told me, but I'm sure he was, especially at that point in his life. She was right. She lived on the island and understood that there was no point in putting their lives on hold. Some things are not meant to be."

"So we shouldn't fight for what we want?"

"Quite the opposite. You should always fight for what you want, but you should also understand that not everything is within your control."

I became pensive for a moment. Then, I examined my iPhone. Paulo had sent me another text message. I had lost count of how many messages he had sent me. My aunt must have noticed.

"A message from him?"

I nodded.

"When are you planning to respond? What are you afraid of?"

"I'm not afraid. Our relationship is over. There are conditions I can't accept."

"Lena, you should call him back and see what he wants. It's the mature thing to do."

I glanced at my phone and began to type while my grandaunt watched me.

"I'm at my grandfather's. I will call you later after I leave."

"It's important I see you," he texted back a couple of minutes later. "Can we meet at the Starbucks across International Plaza?"

"Okay. I'll be there in about an hour. I'll wait for you," I texted.

Tía Rita watched me send and receive messages in silence.

"Well?" she said.

"I'm meeting him."

"Good."

"My parents don't like him. You know that."

"Is it that important to you who they like? What do you want?"

"I want a family. I also want peace. Every time he and I visited my parents after we left, I had to listen to my mother on the phone telling me that she wanted me to marry a Cuban man. She was also making him feel very uncomfortable. That was not fair to him."

"Listen, I will not tell you how to live your life, but watch for those signs that present themselves when we least expect them. Different people come in and out of our lives for a reason. Find that reason, and you will find the correct path to follow."

Chapter 16

The Meeting

When I entered the Starbucks, nervous to see him again weeks after our breakup, my hands turned clammy. Toward the entrance, a man and a woman worked on their laptops while sipping iced coffee. Then, at the end, sitting in one of the cushioned blue chairs, his legs on the matching ottoman, I saw him reading something on his iPad. I walked toward him with uncertain steps. He looked up when he sensed my presence, and our eyes met.

He rose to his feet, and his eyes crinkled with a smile. His skin looked tanner than the last time I saw him; maybe it was his white polo shirt, which revealed his biceps. I extended my hand awkwardly toward him. What was I doing? I swallowed. He took a couple of steps toward me and opened his arms to embrace me. I gave him a friendly embrace, but the moment I touched his broad shoulders and smelled his musky cologne, my legs weakened.

"Thank you for coming," he said. "I saved you a chair. Can I get you something?"

"Sure. Iced coffee with oat milk."

"What size? A Venti as usual?"

I nodded.

"I'll order it."

I sat on the chair next to his as he walked up to the counter. He returned after placing the order, moved the round wooden table between our chairs to one side, and pulled his chair closer to mine.

"I'm sorry I have been calling you so much, but something happened, and I must tell you." His smile disappeared, and he looked distraught.

"Is everything okay?" I asked, moving forward in my seat.

"You know that I have been trying to bring my parents..."

"Yes, I know."

"My mom won't be able to come."

"Why?"

"She died," he said, trying to hold his tears at bay.

"Oh my God!" I replied, bringing my hand to my chest. "How?"

"Covid-19."

"Oh no! Are you okay? What kind of stupid question is that? Of course, you are not okay. I know how much she meant to you. I am so sorry. Why didn't you leave me a message?"

"I needed to tell you in person because this changes everything."

"What do you mean?"

He inhaled deeply and waited a few seconds before replying, then spoke with a calm voice.

"I have thought a lot about my own life since she died. I have thought a lot about us. You said you were breaking up with me because I didn't want a family. Well,... things have changed. Her death made me realize that life is a gift worth fighting for and that I don't want my life to end with me. Now, like you, I want a family. If you'll have me back, I would like to have that family with you."

"I don't know what to say."

"You don't have to say anything now. Just think about it. I know it's a lot to take in. There is also the situation with your parents. They, well, your mother just doesn't like me. I cannot change where I'm from. I'm also not book smart, not the way you are, but my business is doing well. I can offer you a comfortable life. If you want our children to hold on to your roots, I'm not opposed to that. They can be Cuban, Brazilian, and American, all at once."

His eyes glistened as he said this. A tear trickled down my face.

"I... I need to go."

"And your coffee?"

"I can't stay... I'll call you."

Customers were coming in as I was walking out, and looked at me as I rushed out of the establishment. I needed to get away.

Chapter 17

November 1, 1979

AAfter I left Paulo at the Starbucks, I thought about Tía Rita. I needed to speak to her. She was the most understanding and least judgmental person in my family. I called her cell, but she didn't pick up. I thought about calling Maggie. However, she was still studying for the CPA exam, so I decided to go back to my apartment.

I felt so embarrassed about storming out of the Starbucks.

"I'm sorry again about your mom. I'm sorry I left so abruptly," I texted Paulo while waiting at a red light.

No response. A few minutes later, after getting to my apartment, I wrote back.

"Did you get my message?"

Again, no response. I understood. I blew it. He poured his soul out, left it exposed in the open, and I had stepped all over it. I deserved his silence.

My apartment felt empty. I poured myself a glass of water and inserted a pumpkin spice coffee pod into my Keurig coffee maker. I drank the water as I waited for the coffee to brew. Moments later, its aroma filled the room. It felt comforting.

I considered going to the gym. A workout would do me good. Instead, I headed for the living room with a mug full of coffee, set the cup on the end table, and retrieved the box of letters from the cabinet beneath my television set.

I sat on the reclining leather chair and began to read the next letter.

Dear Rolando,

It has been so long since I sent you my last letter: September 15, 1971. I remember it well because I wrote it when my family was in the living room celebrating Papi's birthday. After months had passed and I hadn't received a response from you, I realized you had moved on.

I have thought about you through the years, wondering what would have happened if things had been different. It is such a waste of time to think about 'what if' when there is nothing we can do to change our circumstances.

Recent developments in Cuba have prompted me to write to you. I didn't have your address, but I visited your aunt the other day, and she gave it to me. I hope I wrote it down correctly and that you receive this letter.

So much has happened in the last few years. I was married to Carlos six months after my last letter to you. We had a girl in 1972 and a boy in 1973. My children made my life meaningful again despite everything crumbling around me, literally and metaphorically. Carlos moved into my parents' house on Zapote Street because there is a lack of housing for young couples, and multiple generations often must live together. When I was pregnant, a piece of the ceiling fell while I was cutting some onions in the kitchen, and it nearly killed me.

Carlos "managed" to find the materials needed to repair it. I hope you understand what this entailed, given that the government owns everything. No need to go into details. That showed me how much he cared about me. I didn't think it was possible to fall in love again, but his kindness and generosity made it easy for me to find what I never thought I would after you left. I hope you, too, have found love.

Time here has stood still in many ways, but the paranoia that dominates the country hasn't. It continues to escalate. The government keeps telling us that we must be prepared for when the Americans come to attack us. So, to prepare for that day that never comes, we are asked to stand on street corners at night to watch for antirevolutionary activity.

Someone is always watching us. The person in charge of the Committee of Defense of the Revolution on our block is intrusively involved in people's lives, watching what everyone does and who comes in and out of the houses.

On those days when Fidel Castro speaks at the Plaza de la Revolución, someone comes knocking on every door to make sure we go to the plaza to listen to him. The speeches are always the same: about the "achievements" of the revolution and the "threats of the imperialists" up north.

November 1, 1979

Although Carlos works at a grocery store and has connections, the ratios we are entitled to buy don't always come to the store, so we have to buy food on the black market. When I was pregnant, sometimes I had to eat a piece of bread sprinkled with oil and salt for lunch.

And changing the subject, I hope you were able to recover from your time in the war. As I mentioned earlier, I have often thought about you over the years. In fact, I kept your letters and occasionally read them.

Carlos gets jealous of how I feel about you, but he understands I cannot simply erase that part of my life, just like I cannot erase the love I found with him.

And talking about the changes I mentioned at the beginning of my letter, did you hear about Los Viajes de la Comunidad (trips of the community)? Cubans who live in the United States can now visit their relatives again. I know you have an aunt here. Any plans to visit? If you do, please see us. Bring your family. It would be wonderful to reconnect.

By the way, I never finished college. I figured, what's the point? We have the most educated taxi drivers in this hemisphere. Many of my friends who work with tourists make more than professionals.

As for me, I work as a teacher. Even though I never finished college, the government was so desperate for teachers after the mass exodus in the 1960s that they made it much easier to become a teacher. I don't make much, but at least it gives me something to do.

November 1, 1979

I wish I didn't have to raise my children here. They are being taught to be good communists, to wear red scarves around their necks, and to recite communist slogans.

I probably said more than I should. Write to me if you can.

A hug to you and your family,

Maylin

I put the letter away while I thought about a sentence that, for some reason, had resonated in my mind:

It is such a waste of time to think about 'what if' when there is nothing we can do to change our circumstances.

Chapter 18

April 20, 1980

I thought about putting the box of letters away. Instead, I retrieved the next one. It was also from Maylin.

Dear Rolando,

I was so glad to meet your wife and your two daughters at Christmas. My children enjoyed the time they spent with you. Thank you so much for taking us to the pizzeria and for letting us eat ice cream at Coppélia. My girl loves the outfits your wife brought her. I had to keep reminding her to wear them only on special occasions, but she had never had outfits as pretty as those. She loves the doll, too, while my son doesn't want to play with the firetruck you brought him. He doesn't want it to break, so he keeps it on top of the nightstand.

Please say hello to your beautiful family. Your wife is a lovely person, and I was glad to see you were happy.

So much has happened this past month. I think that the trips of exiles back to the island after so many years led in part to what happened. Exiles seemed to live so much better than those who stayed behind. So, on April 4, the unthinkable occurred. Tired of the deteriorating conditions and the lack of freedom, a group of people crashed a bus through the gates of the Peruvian Embassy in Havana to request political asylum. Police immediately engulfed the area. As you are aware, the government controls the news, so the details are somewhat unclear. A dialogue between the officials at the embassy and Cuban authorities must have taken place, but it didn't have the intended consequences because, suddenly, the guards at the embassy retired. I think it is because the embassy would not give up those who had broken in. Soon after, thousands flooded its ground, asking for political asylum.

The rumors in my neighborhood roamed every street. A group of neighbors gathered at Laura's house. You must remember her. Her husband left in 1968. In 1970, she tried to kill herself after the government stopped allowing people to leave, and she stayed here in Cuba with her three small children. They have been separated for eleven years. Eleven years of watching those children grow up without their father. People wanted to know if she planned to go to the embassy, but she didn't want to.

After a long discussion with me, my husband decided to join the people at the embassy. He thinks that is the only way we will have to leave Cuba one day, even if he has to leave first. He didn't want to risk our children. My brother, who was of military age and the reason why we did not leave, joined my husband. I am so scared for both of them.

A few days after the break-in, Castro appeared on television and stated that anyone with family in the United States could come by boat to the Port of Mariel to pick them up. We don't have any family abroad, but hopefully, my husband and my brother will be successful in somehow getting to the United States or anywhere else.

I am sorry that I am telling you these things. I need to tell someone. I still consider you a very dear friend.

Give your family a big hug from me. Love them and care for them. Now that my husband has been away for a few days, his absence is palpable in every corner. The children and I miss him so much.

I will update you when I know something.

Hugs,

Maylin

Maylin's letter left me at the edge of my seat, thinking about her brother and her husband. I could not stop now. I had to read the next letter.

Chapter 19

May 31, 1980

Dear Rolando,

I hope you and your family are doing well. I wanted to let you know that my husband never made it to the United States. He and my brother were separated while they were at the Port of Mariel. My brother arrived in Miami. A relative of one of his friends who also asked for political asylum called to tell me he was okay, but no one knew anything about my husband. They gave his name to immigration officials to check if he arrived. They could not find him.

According to my brother, my husband left Cuba on April 26, 1980, during a stormy night. It's possible he died at sea, but I want to hold on to the hope that he is still alive. I need to remain hopeful for the children and to keep my sanity. To have found love and lost it twice in my life is more than I can bear.

This is a short letter. I can't write anymore. Hugs to you and your family.

Maylin

May 31, 1980

I examined the letter. In parts of it, the writing was smudged. Perhaps my grandfather's tears. Maybe hers. For years, I had spoken to Maylin, but not once had she mentioned this part of her past. She had always been polite and kind. If I had known her story, perhaps I would have been nicer to her. Her letters were showing me that no one truly knows what crosses others carry.

I consulted my iPhone. Still, no reply from Paulo. I was ready for another letter.

Chapter 20

June 30, 1987

Dear Rolando,

I can't believe that my daughter is turning fifteen this year. Please thank your wife for the beautiful dresses and the money she sent. She is so kind. My children miss their father. I wish he had been still alive to dance with my daughter during her fifteenth birthday celebration. Instead, I will dance with her. No one can ever take her father's place.

I miss Carlos so much. By now, I know I will never find him. He probably drowned at sea. I just hope he didn't suffer. My son looks so much like his father, and it makes me happy to see that part of my husband still lives in my son. Great kid. He is very resourceful, too, when things break around the house.

So many times, I have wished that I could have raised my children elsewhere. Since they turned thirteen, every year, they have been obligated to work in the fields for forty-five days. As a parent, I have no right to tell the government that I don't want my children to be away from me or work for free. I feel so lonely and helpless when they are sent away. When it's their time to work in the fields, with the money you and my brother send me, I buy condensed milk on the black market and cook it in the pressure cooker. Then I travel to the countryside to bring them food. I have to take several buses and walk long distances with a heavy load. At least I know they won't go hungry. They don't like the rice with weevils they serve at the camp.

My son has adapted better than my daughter to be away from home for weeks at a time, in part because he doesn't care about fulfilling the quotas the government assigns to them. She does because she would like to go to college one day and wants to have a good record.

I haven't told you this, but after the Mariel exodus ended, Cuba became unrecognizable. Garbage was allowed to pile up in the streets. So many people had left, over 125,000, that there was no one to pick it up. The government would send trucks to neighborhoods to beat up those who wanted to leave Cuba. Someone was beaten to death in Havana during that time.

I also didn't tell you that Laura and her three children all left during the Mariel boatlift. Remember? I told you that she had been kept separated from her husband for years. Her sister, who lived in the same house with her husband and two daughters, didn't leave right away. Her husband, being an engineer, was forced to work in the park, cutting grass with a machete, only because he wanted to leave the country. He also had to pick up the garbage that had piled up after the Mariel exodus. I was happy when they were finally able to leave in 1982. An old woman lives in their house now.

By the way, with the money you sent us, I will organize a small celebration for my daughter at home. I will send you pictures. She is very excited about her fifteenth birthday.

Hugs to you and your family,

Maylin

I took a sip of coffee. It was getting cold. I grabbed the next letter, but the paper was different, and so was the handwriting. It didn't match Maylin's or my grandfather's. I began to read.

Chapter 21

October 1, 1994

Dear Maylin,

You will probably be surprised to see my letter. You might think, "Why is the wife of the love of my life writing to me?" However, the circumstances have changed, and this time, I need your help.

I have heard about the situation in Cuba after the fall of the Soviet Union. People go hungry on the island, eat cats, and drink water and sugar for breakfast. The Soviet Union subsidized Cuba's economy heavily, and now that those subsidies have dried up, the people are suffering more than ever before.

The "Special Period" has been devastating, so much so that earlier this year, on the 5th of August, hundreds of Cubans gathered at the Explanada de la Punta in Havana and, for the first time, protested against the system. They lost their fear. I think they called this event El Maleconazo. Of course, police took control of the area, and the massive exodus by rafts escalated.

This is the reason for my letter. I know how much you loved my husband. I could tell the love that still existed between the two of you when we met in Havana. Here is my proposal. I have been diagnosed with an aggressive form of cancer. It may last a year or two. I don't know. I am sending you some money with a friend, so you can find a way to get out with your family. Please don't risk your life. Ensure the boat is equipped with a motor. This money will allow you to buy all the supplies you need to come here. The United States has a policy of "dry-foot-wet-foot." That's what we call it. This policy allows Cubans to stay once they reach land.

About my illness, I know that my husband will be too broken without me. He needs stability. The war and all the things that happened in his life impacted him greatly. When I met him, I knew he was a broken man. I fell in love with him the moment I saw him and wanted to fix him. I think I patched him up enough so he could function, but my time with him is coming to an end. I thank God for the years we had together, for my daughters, and for the granddaughter Lena, who I will not see grow up because of this illness that is slowly robbing me of my life. She will need a grandmother. Who better than you?

Please bring this letter and all the letters my husband has sent you through the years. It will be a testimony of the indestructible force of a love that no political system can destroy. In the end, love is all we have. It always wins.

October 1, 1994

As a woman who is at the end of her life, I must confess I was jealous of the love the two of you shared. I uncovered some letters you had sent him that he kept. I asked him to preserve them, as you were an important part of his life. And who knows? Maybe you will be again.

Please take care of yourself. I hope I will still be alive by the time you get here. Send your children a hug. Their father died at sea trying to set them free. Now, I hope that God allows me to finish his mission.

Hugs and blessings,

Matilda

I had never seen this letter from my grandmother. To read her words filled my eyes with emotion. How could she have loved so much to be able to do this? What happened next? I needed to know.

I called Tía Rita again. This time, she answered. I needed to see her, but first, I decided to read the last letter.

Chapter 22

The Last Letter

I retrieved the last letter with anticipation. I recognized the writing. It was Maylin's. I leaned back and began to read:

December 15, 1994

Dear Matilda,

I cried so much when I read your letter, and as much as I would like to bring my family to freedom, I do not want to do it at your expense. I promise I will repay your family the money you have sent me.

I am praying every day that doctors find a cure and are able to bring you back to health. The United States is so advanced, so please don't lose hope. You must fight for life. Don't forget that miracles happen every day. I'm sure you have seen many during your career as a nurse.

If something were to happen to you, I promise to be Rolando's friend. Too many years have passed, and neither one of us is the same person. I love him now like a dear friend. I also love the years we had together and the illusions of youth we shared. We had so many dreams smashed by time and politics, but we both managed to rebuild our lives. I'm his past. You are his present. However, rest assured that if there is anything I can do to help him and his family, I will. That is the least I can do.

I know you don't have brothers or sisters. However, if I am able to make it to the United States, I will care for you as a sister.

Imagining my husband's last hours of life in the middle of the ocean with no one to help him makes me fear for my own life and the lives of my children. I hear that so many of my countrymen have died at sea. But my children insist we must risk it all; they say staying here is no longer an option.

They inherited their father's fearlessness and determination.

My son has already started to secure what's needed for our trip, but I have mixed feelings about leaving. This old house is all I know. Inside its walls are the memories of my parents, the happy memories of my first years of marriage, and the birth of my children. Every corner of it reminds me of a happy moment, and to think I will never see it again shakes me to the core. Also, I never envisioned freedom without my husband. I feel so lost without him.

My daughter turned twenty-four this year. The children are making me feel so old. Her boyfriend wants to come with us. God knows we will need his help. He is a fisherman and knows about navigation. Amazing how some people come into our lives at those precise times when they are needed most.

Well, I have said enough. I don't want to bore you with all my ramblings, and I need to get dinner ready. I will pray for God to guide me in making the right decisions and to help my doctors find a cure for my illness.

A big hug to you and your beautiful family.

Maylin

I finished reading the last letter, and I felt a strange feeling inside. There was so much insight into the human condition, the passage of time, and the impact of the decisions we make. They made me realize that I was at a critical crossroads in my own life, a fork in the road. I just didn't know which way to go.

Chapter 23

Grandma Matilda

Tía Rita and I sat in the living room of my grandfather's house and looked at old pictures from a brown photo album. Meanwhile, my grandfather, sitting in his rocking chair, read an issue of the Economist magazine and glanced at us once in a while. It was not the first time I had seen that album, but now that I knew my grandfather's story through the love letters I had read, the pictures gained more meaning. The old album made me think about how much time had changed. In 2021, no one kept pictures in photo albums anymore, but on Facebook, Instagram, Twitter, and iPhones. What would happen if social media and iPhones ceased to exist? As remote as that notion appeared, it was still within the realm of possibilities.

"These are your grandparents when they got married at St. Joseph's Church. Your grandfather looked so thin back then."

"Why is everyone calling me fat all the time?" Grandpa protested. Tía Rita rolled her eyes and ignored him.

"Grandma Matilda was so beautiful. I love her long, wavy brown hair. And she had the eyes of a kind woman. Now, from reading the letters, I know just how much she cared for Grandpa."

"I was lucky to have her in my life, especially right after the war," he said.

"Reading her letter felt as if she was talking from beyond the grave. It helped me see her kindness. Also, knowing your history allows me to appreciate you so much more."

"Oh, so you didn't appreciate me before?" my grandfather said, looking at me over his glasses.

"You know what I mean. By the way, I don't know if you noticed that I left the box of letters on top of the dining room table when I arrived. You were in the bathroom."

"You can keep those letters," he said.

"I can?"

"Yes. You will be the family historian. Every family needs one of those."

"Thank you so much. I promise to take care of them. I do have a question."

"What else do you want to know? You know more about me now than my daughter."

"Were you happy with my grandmother?"

Without hesitation, he replied, "Matilda made me very happy. She was a caring and thoughtful wife and mother. As a nurse at the VA hospital, she had witnessed a great deal. Yet, she never allowed those experiences to impact her family, even though sometimes I would find her crying in the bathroom when she had lost a patient. It wasn't always easy for her to separate her role as a nurse from her role as a human being."

"That probably made her a great nurse."

"That she was."

"Where was she born?"

"She was born in Havana, but her father moved the family to the United States when she was five. He was in the retail business, mainly in clothing stores. Her mother died of cancer when she was twelve. That's why she went into healthcare."

"Did her father remarry?"

"When she was fifteen, he did, but she never got along with her stepmother, a woman who was much younger than her father. She never had any brothers and sisters from her father's first marriage. Her stepmother, however, had a baby boy when she was seventeen. She didn't feel as loved by her father after that, and at eighteen, she moved out and shared an apartment with friends. To be able to work and put herself through school with practically no support system tells you the kind of person she was."

"Grandpa, did you and Grandma ever visit the friends you met in Vietnam?"

"Not with your grandmother. That came much later after Matilda died."

I was too little when Grandma Matilda left us. So, I didn't remember her, except through pictures.

After we finished looking at the pictures, Tía Rita said Grandma Matilda waited for Maylin and her family to arrive from Cuba.

Maylin's boat had broken at sea, and she and her family almost didn't make it. Luckily, a group of fishermen found them just in time to save their lives. Maylin was grateful that, thanks to Matilda, Carlos's dream of his family living in the United States had materialized. Maylin showed her gratitude by visiting my grandmother at least twice a week as she began her new life in America.

"The hospital did everything they could to save her," Tía Rita said. "She was like family to everyone she met, but in the end, her doctors lost the battle. Matilda died less than a year after her initial diagnosis. When she died, your grandfather, your mom, and your uncle were by her side."

Maylin and her children had also come to visit a few hours before my grandmother took her last breath.

During Maylin's visit, my grandmother asked everyone to step out of the room for a moment. She wanted to speak to Maylin alone. Maylin later told my grandfather about their conversation.

"The end is near," she said. "Promise me you will be by Rolando's side. He will need you."

Maylin promised she would.

A few months after she arrived from Cuba, Maylin found a job at the business office of a glass company owned by one of my grandfather's friends. She and my grandfather were good friends at first. My mother was jealous of her. She didn't want anyone to take my grandmother's place, but after watching her father fall apart several times in front of her, she asked Maylin to help him. Over time, their relationship evolved, and my mother reluctantly accepted her.

Three years after my grandmother Matilda died, my grandfather and Maylin got married during a small ceremony at Tampa's courthouse. Maylin then became Nana, the only grandmother I remembered. After reading the letters and learning about the love that existed between my grandfather and Maylin, I now understood why, at times, my mother seemed to resent Nana.

During holidays, Maylin prepared big meals for the entire family, hers from her first marriage and ours. She brought so much joy to the celebrations, but there were times I found my mother lost in her thoughts.

After Maylin and my grandfather retired, they bought a small RV and traveled all over the United States, visiting the places my grandfather had heard about during the war. He was even able to reconnect with some of his friends. Grandpa and Nana would send us postcards of every city they visited: New Orleans, Birmingham, San Francisco, Chicago, Austin, and so many others. I lost count.

They had misadventures, too, like when his RV broke down in the Smokey Mountains and they had a close encounter with a black bear. Another time, someone tried to break into the RV in the middle of the night. They were both asleep, but footsteps outside the RV awoke my grandfather. He always carried a weapon with him and knew how to defend himself, so he won the altercation with the intruder. In fact, his story made it to the local newspapers.

My grandfather and Nana would send me teddy bears from different cities, even though I was already an adult. I had a full collection that I kept next to that first brown bear he had given me.

"So, tell me what's going on with your life. Any boyfriends?"—my grandfather asked.

"No, Grandpa."

"I don't want to get involved in anybody's business, but life is meant to be shared. This new generation, raised in this country, hasn't experienced enough hardship. I fear for this generation. Now this pandemic hits, and they are not ready."

"They will figure things out," Tía Rita said. "Remember that no one learns from the experiences of others."

"Maybe people should," I said. "I think I learned from my grandfather's letters."

"I hope so," he said, leaning his chin between his index and middle fingers. "Tell me if I'm wrong. Your mother is trying to connect you with Mark, and Paulo keeps calling you to get back to you. At least he was calling you until recently," he said.

"How do you know?"

"I'm old, not deaf."

"What should I do?"

"Only you can decide," Tía Rita said.

"I think I blew it with Paulo."

"Paulo is a real man, the kind of man you don't play with," Grandpa said. "He has looked at the devil in the eye like I did during the war."

"What do you mean?" I asked.

"I talked to him about his life. There are things he shared with me that helped me understand that you won't be able to push him around like a toy. The day you disappoint him, he will turn his back on you, and you will never see him again."

My eyes flashed wide open.

"When you said he has looked at the devil in the eye, to what are you referring?"

My grandfather took a deep breath.

"He witnessed his brother's brutal murder when he was a child. There is nothing worse than watching someone you care for be killed without you being able to do anything to stop it. That haunts you for the rest of your life."

I covered my mouth with my hand. "He never told me."

"Real men don't like being perceived as weak."

"Vulnerable and weak are two different things," I said.

"Not the way I see it."

"I don't know how to fix this."

"You said you learned something from my letters. What did you learn?"

"That we can't really make plans as circumstances beyond our control can change those plans in the blink of an eye."

"Is that all you learned?"

"I learned that sometimes life can give us a second chance."

"Just be aware that second chances are not guaranteed. Sometimes, they never come." He paused for a moment, then added, "Anything else?"

"Is this a quiz?"

"Just making sure you were paying attention."

"I learned about the power of love. I learned about what people are willing to do for love."

"Okay," he said and adjusted his glasses again. "We seem to be getting somewhere."

"So, I must ask myself, am I in love? And if so, what am I willing to do for love?"

He remained silent.

"I must go now," I said, rising to my feet.

"Where are you going?" Tía Rita asked.

"I will call you later. I have something to do."

"Don't forget to take the letters," my grandfather said.

Chapter 24

My Parents

MMy mother was in the laundry room folding clothes when I arrived. She wore a sleeveless pink blouse and fitted beige pants that accentuated her curves. Although in her forties, she looked younger than her age. She couldn't stay still, always doing something around the house, even after my father would ask her to sit down next to him and watch television. She would comply at first, then wait for his first signs of boredom. When in the middle of whatever they were watching, he reached out to his iPad and began surfing through Facebook; that was her clue. She would get up and announce she had forgotten to do something.

"But we were watching this program together," he would say.

"You are not watching anything! You are on Facebook. You do Facebook, and I'll do something around the house. It's not going to clean itself."

My mother stopped doing her chores and turned toward me with open arms.

"Hello, sweetheart. How nice of you to stop by. It feels like you are always either at work, with friends, or at your grandfather's."

I kissed her on the cheek, and she reciprocated and caressed my arm.

"Sometimes, it's hard to make time. I need to do better."

"That's okay. I understand. I'm not used to seeing you all grown up. For me, you will always be a little girl."

"I know, Mami." I placed my head on hers, which was pulled back in a ponytail, the first signs of darker roots appearing on her blond hair partition.

"Can I give you some rice pudding?"

"No, thanks. I need to watch my diet."

"You are so worried about your figure, but you look lovely." She caressed my brown hair. "Well, let's go to the living room."

"Is Papi here?"

"He went to Publix to pick up some milk and eggs, but he'll be back soon."

"Good. It's best if we talk alone. It's important."

"Is everything okay?"

"Yes, I just want to talk to you. That's all."

"You're scaring me. You're not pregnant, are you?"

"No, I'm not pregnant."

"Thank God. I would never want my daughter to get pregnant before marriage. That would be sacrilegious."

I took a deep breath, and we walked to the living room. We sat next to each other on the sofa.

"I forgot to tell you," she said. "Julio called."

"Uncle Julio?"

"I don't know why you insist on calling him 'Uncle Julio.' He is Maylin's son. He is not our blood."

"He has always treated me like family. Stop being so jealous."

"Jealous? Me?" She pointed at her chest while her brows, compressed, met over her eyes. When I remained silent, she softened her expression, elevated her head slightly, and added, "Anyhow, changing to a related topic: Your grandfather wants all the family reunited this Christmas. I tell him that it's still too soon. This pandemic has not gone away. But he insists. He tells me he may not be around next year. His way of getting me to do what he wants."

"Sounds like someone I know. So, who's coming?"

"Well, I had to invite Maylin's family, her son and daughter, and their families. And guess what? Julio has one more kid from another woman who showed up unexpectedly."

"Another one?"

"This is kid number five. I don't know how his wife can tolerate so many children from so many different women. He's trying to create his own United Nations. Most of these kids he had when he was a teenager and went to clubs, sleeping with everything that caught his eye. Some of the women were married."

"How do they know it's his kid if they were sleeping around?"

"Some just knew. Some could do a better job of hiding it from their husbands than others. He had a child with a Russian, a Chinese, an Irishwoman, his Cuban wife, and the most recent addition is Nigerian."

"Nigerian?"

"Yes, DNA-tested like the others."

"A girl or a boy?"

"A beautiful young woman. She's twenty-three and attending Harvard Law."

"And they are all going to be here for Christmas?"

"They are. All five children! That wife of his is a saint."

"Talking about DNA, I did mine through 23andMe."

"Why would you do that?"

"I wanted to know my ethnicity."

"You didn't have to do a test for that. I could've told you that. You are of Spanish descent. No mystery there."

I giggled.

"Well. When are you going to show me the results?" she asked.

"A little later. First, I wanted to talk to you about something else."

"What?"

"Paulo."

She rolled her eyes. "I thought the two of you broke up."

"Yes, but I broke up with him because I was tired of hearing you look down on him and criticize him."

"You never said anything."

"No, you are right. That has been my problem all along. I never say anything. You know, recently, I read the letters my grandfather kept for so many years."

"What letters?"

"Letters between Maylin and him."

"I never knew about any letters."

"Then, you don't know Grandpa like I do. His letters taught me so much. They taught me to fight for what I want. And I will."

"Why are you looking at me like that?"

"How?"

"Like I'm your enemy. All I have done is love you and want the best for you. I don't want us to disappear. I don't want who we are, who my father is, to disappear. That will happen if you marry someone who is not like us."

"You're scared. That's why you don't want me to be with Paulo. I know who I am. Grandpa has always reminded me of that. Remember how many times he played 'La Guantanamera' for me on his guitar while singing along with it? I know almost every song from his generation. I will pass that knowledge on to my children. You don't need to worry about that."

"It's more than that."

"What is it?"

"That man. Have you looked at him? We know very little about him. He's most likely a leftist."

"Mami, he's a bigger capitalist than we are. He built his own business from the ground up. He hired people and made significant contributions to the economy. He is not a socialist."

"Where are his parents from?"

"Brazil is a nation that is a blend of many nations. Why does that matter?"

"We come from Spain, the motherland. We should stick to people who are like us."

I looked down and remained silent for a while. Then, I opened my purse, extracted a folded piece of paper, and gave it to her.

"What's that?"

"My 23andMe results."

She glanced at me with distrust before unfolding it, then quietly read it. I could see her face turning red.

"That's who I am, Mami."

She gave me the paperback.

"Those results must be wrong. You are not 9% Cuban Indian. You don't have Nigerian ancestry."

"How do you know? Have you ever talked to my father about his background?"

We heard the garage door open, and moments later, the side door leading from the garage to the house opened. My father, wearing a blue polo shirt and white shorts that exposed his muscular legs, appeared. He carried two bags of groceries. My mother rose to her feet, took the paper from me, and walked toward my father.

"Alberto, your daughter just gave me this piece of paper showing that she is 8% Nigerian and 9% Cuban-Indian. I thought your family was all from Spain."

My father started laughing while he walked toward the dining room with the groceries. He began to empty the bags with a smile on his face.

"You really thought that?"

He glanced at her, waiting for a response. When she didn't say anything, he stopped what he was doing, pulled a dining room chair, and sat down. My mother sat across from him.

"You told me your grandfather was from Spain," she said, trying to appear calm.

"He was. He fell in love with a woman who was part Cuban Indian and part African. They had my father, who was light-skinned like my grandfather, but seeing how people treated her, my grandmother insisted he marry someone who looked like my grandfather. She didn't want her son to feel what she felt, not to be allowed in parties because his mother was black."

"You never showed me any pictures of her."

"She didn't allow anyone to take her picture."

My eyes filled with tears. "Oh my God, Papi. That's so sad."

My father took a deep breath. "What's this all about?" he asked. "Why all of a sudden has our daughter's DNA become an issue?"

"Your daughter still has feelings for that Brazilian."

"And you don't like him because he doesn't look like us."

"It's not as simple as you put it."

My father looked into her eyes. "I'd better go put these groceries away." Glancing at me, he added, "As far as I am concerned, you can be with whomever you want."

"I thought you agreed with Mami," I said.

"I never said that."

"You never stopped her from making Paulo's life miserable."

"And that's on me. Maybe I should have."

My mother crossed her arms. "So, I'm the bad one now?" She paused for a moment and looked down, arms crossed. "I'm going to my room. I have a headache. As far as I'm concerned, you can do whatever you want. I'm done giving my opinion. I have always wanted what I thought was best for you. Why is that such a bad thing to do? If you want to throw our culture out the window, you do that. I'm done trying!"

My mother stood up and stormed out of the room. Moments later, she slammed the door of the master bedroom.

I grabbed the milk and the eggs from the table and took them to the refrigerator. Then, I sat across from my father.

"What should I do?"

"What do you want to do?"

I stretched my arms over the table. "I don't know. Part of me thinks that there won't be an end to this, that she will always be upset if I stay with Paulo."

"Look, over the three years that you were with that guy, you never asked me anything. I never said anything. All I have done is work to give you the best life I could give you. I don't think I made a mistake. I think I gave you too much. You just don't know how to fight for what you want. You are used to everything being handed to you."

"My God, Papi. Tell me how you truly feel."

"It's true, my princess. That was my mistake. Do you love that guy?"

"I do. I have from the moment I saw him."

"Do you think he loves you?"

"He does."

"What are you waiting for? I empathize with Paulo. Your maternal grandfather, Paulo, and I share one thing. And Lena, don't look at me that way. Your grandfather told me what Paulo had shared with him. I know he watched his brother's murder. His brother was stabbed multiple times by a gang when Paulo was a child. Like your grandfather and me, he has looked at death in the face."

"You?"

"Yes, when I left Cuba, and our boat broke. We were at sea for days. Food ran out. Then the water ran out. One of the guys who came on the boat with me, like all of us, started to see visions, things that weren't there. And he just jumped. He jumped in the water and disappeared. None of us had enough energy to go after him. If it had not been for a boat of fishermen that passed by, I would not be here telling you this story."

"Maylin had a similar experience, but I don't understand how that story applies to my situation."

"The point is that all three of us share that bond. We speak the same language. We are survivors. People like us can love with all of our hearts, but we can as easily walk away because we try at all costs to defend ourselves from pain. It's a defense mechanism. Do what's right for you, no matter what your mother says. No matter what anyone says. You are a grown woman, working, paying your rent, and even helping your grandfather. You have a good heart. Follow your heart."

I went around the table and hugged my father. "Thank you, Papi."

"Women sometimes make life so complicated."

I giggled. "I'm sorry. I didn't mean to make things difficult for you."

"That's okay. I will just stay out of her way until she is ready to talk."

I thought about saying goodbye to my mother, but she needed time alone, and so did I.

Chapter 25

Dinner for Two

For a week, I had not heard from Paulo, even though I had texted him a few times. His silence was worse than if he had told me not to bother him again, and so was the emptiness I found when I returned to my apartment after working all day. I needed to break my routine.

Maggie's passing of two parts of her CPA exam was the perfect opportunity to do something different. To celebrate, one night, I invited her to the Columbia Restaurant in historic Ybor City for dinner, a place where Paulo and I had been a few times, his favorite restaurant. I realized the moment I walked into the packed place and listened to the laughter and lively conversations that I should have gone elsewhere.

Before, when Paulo and I were dating, I would have been happy to come to Columbia. The historic building where it was housed, built in 1905, had never failed to make me feel at home. The world's largest Spanish restaurant was a gem of Spanish architecture, from its elaborate tiles to its inner courtyard, surrounded by arched balconies. This was our favorite part of the restaurant, but during my visit with Maggie, when the waiter walked us to that area, I asked him to take us to the opposite side, near the bar.

"This part is so beautiful," Maggie said, all dressed up for the occasion in a black cocktail dress.

I had no option but to stay.

"So, how are the Christmas preparations going?" she asked after we ordered our drinks.

"You know my mother, stressed out as always, wondering where she is going to accommodate everyone, including all of Julio's children, five as of the newest arrival."

"Five? Where is this last one from?"

"The young woman is of Nigerian descent. Five children and five mothers. What was he doing before he finally married his Cuban wife, populating the world? And I don't know how she accepts children from every part of the world popping out when she least expects it."

"It sounds like you will have a great party, but your mom is right. Where are you going to accommodate all those people?"

"My parents own a four-bedroom house in the Country Place subdivision in Carrollwood, and they live, as you know, near the Country Place Park, so some of the family will park there and walk to the house, which is only about a block away. Some of our neighbors will have their cars in the garage and will let us use their spaces. My father is very resourceful and is turning his large backyard into the venue for the party."

"They may need to request special permission at the park if they plan to keep cars there after hours."

"It is a neighborhood park, but I'm sure my mother is handling all of those details."

"I love big families. That sounds so exciting. Your Nana used to hold those big celebrations, and now your mom continues the tradition."

"Well, last year, with COVID in full swing, we skipped Christmas, other than for a small dinner at home. Also, Nana had just died. I think that's why my grandfather came up with the idea to do something big this year in her honor."

"It will be wonderful, I'm sure, especially if your grandfather plays his guitar."

"You know he will. He loves to sing Cuban songs on his acoustic guitar."

"Your grandfather sounds like a very special person," she said. I nodded and brought a smile back. She began to examine the courtyard and the balconies above it. "I love this restaurant. It is breathtaking."

"I thought you had been here before."

"No, it's my first time. I always saw the building but never went inside." She paused and started to look through the menu. "So, what do you recommend?"

"The paella is excellent, and so is the pollo salteado, which is Paulo's favorite dish here."

"What is that last one?"

"It's chicken sautéed with Spanish sausage, potatoes, and delicious spices. So good. It's served with yellow rice, but Paulo always orders plantains to go along with it."

"Sounds like a winner. I will have that."

"I will, too."

"Have you heard anything from him?"

"No, I have texted him a few times. Nothing. I blew it. My grandfather was right. He's a real man. I played with his feelings, and I lost him."

"I'm sorry. I really am."

"Me too. But anyhow, let's talk about you. When are you sitting for the next two parts of the exam?"

"I'm taking a little break. A week or two, and then the heavy studying begins. I can't wait to get it all done."

"And then, you will have a lot of options in terms of jobs."

"That's the idea. I am starting to connect with people in companies where I would like to work after I finish."

"That's great. Perhaps I should pursue a master's degree in accounting. It will give me something to do. Besides, my employer has tuition reimbursement."

"I think you should, Lena. Your father would be very proud."

"I know he would. I need to get motivated."

"I'll be your motivation," she said. "Come on, you can do it. It's like your father says, 'a year or two of hard work for a lifetime of rewards.' You can't go wrong."

"You're probably right. Going back to college will keep my mind occupied."

"Who knows? Maybe you will find the next Paulo?"

"The next Paulo? In an accounting class? I don't think so. Besides, I would never marry an accountant. I need some happiness in my life."

"That's hurtful!" she said.

"I don't mean you! You are not boring, but most guys I know who work as accountants are. It could be just my personal experience and not a reflection of reality."

"I'm sure that the profession has nothing to do with the personality."

"If you say so."

Maggie and I talked throughout the meal. Her company helped me break the routine. I needed that. While we walked back to our cars, she thanked me for dinner and asked me, "Have you considered writing a letter to Paulo?"

"A letter?"

"Yes, like the love letters from Cuba, you read. Well, not only from Cuba, but you know what I mean."

"No, I haven't thought about a letter."

"It might spark his curiosity."

"I don't know. I don't want to come across as desperate."

"But you are!"

"What do you mean?"

"I know I have only known you for three years, but I'm good at analyzing people."

"I didn't realize you had a minor in psychology."

"You are a pain in the rear tonight!"

"So, what have you observed about me?"

"You are miserable. You have no life. You don't know how to restart it. You are drowning in the routine. Well, did I get it right?"

"Maggie, am I that transparent?"

"And some more." She giggled.

"I never considered writing him a letter."

"You should. Tell him how you feel. If it doesn't work, only the time you spend pouring your soul into the letter will be lost."

"I don't know..."

"Think about it."

I hugged Maggie before walking to my car. After getting inside and turning on the ignition, I started to think about her suggestion. Then, I searched for a Spanish-language radio station and cranked it up.

Chapter 26

Letter to Paulo

I tried to remain as busy as possible. Now that I had the option to go into the office, I did. Tired of being home alone, some of my coworkers did too. It was refreshing to see them in person after so long. I went to the gym and worked on my finances. Then, at the end of my day, I also communicated with a cousin who resided in Cuba.

She was one of Grandpa's Facebook friends who had requested my "friendship" the year before. We had only exchanged a handful of messages in "Messenger" about how we were related. After talking about her with my grandfather, I concluded that Esperanza (that's her name) and I were distant cousins. According to my grandfather, distant cousins are still cousins. If someone has our blood, they are family.

After reading the letters, I became more interested in the details of what was happening inside the island, and Esperanza became my conduit and an opportunity to practice my Spanish. She had worked for the electric company for years. In the first half of the year 2021, after the number of COVID cases skyrocketed in Cuba, only essential personnel stayed in the offices, and she began to work a few hours from home. She was tired of being inside her apartment and only going out to stand in line for hours. Esperanza would get up very early and stand in line from five until past noon, only to find that whatever had come to the stores that day had run out.

On Wednesday of the last week of October, she wrote to me, "I have stood in line for several hours during each of the past three days and have not been able to buy anything. I am so tired."

She was in her forties and cared for her grandfather. It became clear to me she needed help, so I went online and found a place that would deliver food to her door. It was expensive, not something I could do every day, but she was so thankful when I told her what I had ordered: thirty eggs, two pounds of chicken, two pounds of pork, and a few pounds of beans. She needed milk, not for her, she said, but for her grandfather. I couldn't find any on the website I used, which someone told me was very reliable. Instead of milk, I bought two pounds of cheese. Helping her made me feel better about my situation.

Things could always be worse, a lot worse.

In the second week of October, I decided to write a letter. It had been several weeks since my last communication with Paulo. I imagined my cousin Marta on his bed and Paulo kissing her the way he used to kiss me. I thought about calling my cousin to see how things were and maybe learn more about what could be going on between her and Paulo. During my vacation, I allowed her to stay at the apartment for one night because guilt consumed me. Like my grandfather said, she was family. During her visit, Maggie stared at me when my cousin went on about how handsome Paulo was. Not that he was truly that handsome, but he exuded manhood and strength. That was what we both liked about him. I should have said to her, "Back off!"

I didn't.

I concluded that if I had any opportunity to become part of his life again, I needed to do something. So, on a Friday afternoon, after I came home from work, I retrieved a yellow pad and began to write:

October 15, 2021

Dear Paulo,

I want to apologize for acting like a spoiled child. I am sorry. You didn't deserve that. So, I did something I should have done from the beginning. I talked to my mother about us. I wanted to understand why she had treated you the way she did. Because I had my suspicions, I sent my saliva to 23andMe for analysis. When I showed Mami my DNA results, which suggested that, although I was from predominantly Spanish descendants, I had close to 20% Cuban-Indian and African roots, her reaction made things clear. She was angry at my father for not disclosing his background to her. I guess I don't really blame her. Her values were passed on from generation to generation.

First, her excuse was that she didn't like your "background," and then that perhaps you were a socialist. My DNA cleared the first issue. If she rejects you for the reasons I think she does, she would have to reject my father and me. Her expression told me she wasn't willing to do that. She looked so conflicted when my father confirmed that my results reflected reality. Regarding her concerns that you might be a socialist, I told the truth. Paulo is more capitalist than we are. You built your own business, hired men, and made a significant contribution to this country. When she had nothing to say, she ran to her room. I do feel bad for her. She has been a great mother despite long-held misconceptions.

My father and my grandfather both admire you. My father had not said anything until the day of my argument with my mother. He expressed his remorse for having kept quiet.

I have visited my parents' house since the argument, but my mother has been busy preparing for the Christmas party, and she hasn't said anything else other than to ask me about you. "Are the two of you back together?" she asked. I said, "No. I think I blew it," and she apologized. She sees how I feel and wishes she could do something about it.

This is my final attempt to get you back into my life. If you don't respond, I will understand. I deserve your silence. Last year, you asked me to marry you. I said I wasn't ready. I am now. If you want us to go downtown and get married there, just the two of us, I will do that too. I have always loved you. That never changed, not even when I broke up with you, because I didn't think it was fair to you to subject you to Mami's constant rejection. I was wrong in not fighting for you then. Lesson learned.

I miss your embraces and your kisses. I miss falling asleep in your arms when my parents thought I had slept in my apartment. I miss being your woman.

Hugs and kisses,

Lena

Chapter 27

Thanksgiving Day

My parents, my grandfather, Tía Rita, and I had a small Thanksgiving celebration at my parents' house. They stuck to the traditional meal: black beans and white rice, turkey stuffed with picadillo (Cuban-style ground beef) and stuffing, fried ripe plantains, tostones for my grandfather, who preferred the green version of plantains, and a salad with plenty of tomatoes and avocado. After holding hands and thanking God for our blessings, I served myself a very small portion of rice, as usual, along with some black beans and turkey, all in moderation.

"If you keep eating like that, you're not going to make it until Christmas," my grandfather said while he served himself double the quantity I had on my plate.

"I'm saving room for the papaya chunks."

"It's not papaya. It's fruta bomba. Call it by the correct name," Tía Rita reminded me. "If I ever used that word in Cuba, my mother would have slapped me."

"Tía Rita, we are not in Cuba. Here, it is just the fruit."

In Cuba, papaya was used in street language to refer to the female genitalia.

"So, how are the Christmas celebrations coming along?"

"A lot of work. Some close friends from our jobs are also coming."

"How many people are you going to stuff into the house?" Tia Rita asked. "The pandemic has not gone away. I'm glad I received my booster. My brother did, too. If the rest of you die, don't say I didn't warn you."

"It's only a couple of friends who don't have family here. And changing the subject, Lena, did our cousin get the last package of food you sent her?"

"Yes, Mami. I forgot to tell you that she thanked everyone. I told her it was a gift from the family. She also sent me a letter through Messenger."

"Now that you are done eating your food, can you read it?" my mother said, serving herself more turkey from a large plate near her.

"But I want to eat dessert first," I protested.

"Not until everyone is done with their dinner," my mother replied.

I looked at my iPhone, selected the Facebook application, and searched for the letter in Messenger. I found it and began to read:

Lena, the deliveryman just dropped off the food you sent me. Please thank our Tampa family. I don't know what we would do without your help. I cannot say too much because of the laws that were passed. I don't want to go to jail for saying negative things. Mamá needs me. She could not do the long lines at her age.

Yesterday, I got up early, stood in line at 5 a.m., and didn't reach the front of the line until past noon, only to find out that the oil had run out. And never mind the milk. I'm glad you sent me some cheese. I will give it to Mamá as a substitute.

Please tell everyone you know to pray for us. So many of us have turned to religion out of desperation. Only a miracle can save us.

Love and kisses,

Your cousin, Esperanza

When I finished reading the letter, my mother grabbed my father's hand and wiped a tear on it. Everyone remained silent for a moment. Finally, my mother said, "We have so much to be thankful for, and yet, we find reasons to be miserable. We have food, a roof over our heads, freedom, and life. When I read letters from our family in Cuba, my heart breaks."

Another long silence followed.

"Well, no more sadness," my grandfather said. "I finished my food, and I want dessert, not only the papaya, as Lena calls it, but I also want a piece of pumpkin pie."

"What about your sugar?" asked Tía Rita.

"First, my two wives, and now you? You see why I didn't invite my lady friend to this celebration?"

"You have a lady friend?" my mother asked.

"See what you made me do?" my grandfather asked Tía Rita. Then, turning to my mother, he added, "I knew you would look at me the way you are looking at me right now. She is just a friend. We connected through Facebook. We used to live in the same neighborhood when we lived in Cuba."

"Invite her to the Christmas party!" my mother said.

"More people?" protested Tia Rita.

We all laughed.

At the end of our meal, my parents began to play old Cuban music and danced with each other.

"I remember when I used to dance," my grandfather would say. "Now, I was a good dancer."

"Are you saying I don't know how to dance?"

"I didn't say that. Stop putting words in my mouth."

The moment she turned around, he whispered to me, "They have no clue."

He never failed to make me laugh. As I did, my mind shifted to Paulo. It had been weeks since we last met. He had not responded to my letter.

Now I knew I had lost him.

Chapter 28

Christmas Preparations

We was only a week away from Christmas, and my parent's house boasted colorful decorations, including a tall Christmas tree in the family room, full of presents beneath—one for each person who was coming.

I enjoyed visiting my parents during the Christmas season. There was always something going on. My mother couldn't help herself. Some people preferred Halloween, others preferred Thanksgiving, and for her, it was Christmas.

I was sitting on the sofa while my father sat in the recliner, trying to watch the sports channel with the volume down. My mother placed one more present under the tree and then sat next to me.

"Why couldn't we do one of those pick-a-number games?" my father asked. "You know how much money you have spent this Christmas? Do you think we are made of money? Don't forget that you married a Cuban refugee."

"I used our credit card points to get $10 gift cards from Starbucks for almost everyone. I bought Dad cologne and a few other things. Nothing extravagant," my mother replied.

"The credit card bill begs to differ!"

"Stop fighting," I said, examining the presents from afar to guess which one was mine. "So, what did you get me?"

"What did we get you? You're too big for presents," my father said mockingly.

I smiled. "Okay, Dad. Don't tell me. So Mami, what are you serving on Christmas?"

"It's going to be a delicious dinner. Roasted pork, *moros* (a mixture of seasoned black beans and rice), plantains, yucca, avocado salad, sweet potato casserole, corn casserole, and ham," my mother said.

"Then, of course, all the desserts, even a cake," my father added. My mother looked at him and opened her eyes wide. "And I forgot! Your mother didn't think we had enough people and invited the priest."

"The priest?" I asked.

"What's wrong with inviting him? God knows we need all the blessings we can get. Besides, your poor grandfather thinks this is his last Christmas."

"So, you are having a priest administer your father's last rites at Christmas. Only your mother could think of such an idea!"

I shook my head. "You guys are always fighting."

"She wants me to lose the little hair I have left," my father said.

"Oh, you love my craziness. Stop acting as if you don't. And before I forget, Lena, given that I want to make this Christmas extra special for your grandfather, we should both wear long dresses."

"Mami, who wears long dresses at Christmas? It's not as if we were attending a gala."

"I want the photographer to get nice pictures of the two of us with your grandfather. It will be a nice memory to have after he is no longer with us."

My father closed the recliner and rose to his feet. He then crossed his arms.

"You hired a photographer for a Christmas party? Lena, please call 911. Your mother needs to be taken to a mental hospital. She has lost her mind!"

"I want to give my father a fancy Christmas party. He thinks this is his last one."

"It will be my last Christmas at the pace you are going!"

"Just sit down and keep watching whatever you're watching, and let me talk to my daughter," she said, then turning to me, she added, "So, sweetheart, like I was saying, let's wear long dresses for Grandpa. Please do it for him. I already paid for the photographer. I want Grandpa to have a special night. He told me he is bringing his guitar and performing for the family."

"Leave it to the Perez family to create the strangest Christmas ever. Lena, you should also bring a bottle of wine. We will both need some to survive your mother's nightmarish Christmas party."

"It will be a nice celebration," my mother said, placing the palms of her hands together.

"If Maylin rose from her grave and came to our Christmas party, she would have a heart attack right there and die again. I guarantee you."

I giggled while watching their interactions. I wondered what it would feel like to have what they had.

No matter what my father said, his expression told me how much he loved my mother. It told me that he would not be who he was without her.

And at that moment, I felt blessed to have both of them in my life.

Chapter 29

Christmas Day

IIt was almost time for the guests to arrive at my parents' house, and my mother sat by the dining room table, signing a couple of Christmas cards.

My father, responsible for creating a party atmosphere in the backyard, had outdone himself. He had arranged two round tables, each accommodating ten people, on either side of a cemented area. Each had white linen tablecloths and tasteful Christmas centerpieces. The chairs all had white linen coverings, giving it more the appearance of a formal affair than a family Christmas gathering.

My grandfather's guitar stood on a stand on the cemented area between the two sets of tables. My father had installed a podium and a cable for a microphone as well. Christmas music played from the speakers. Behind the guitar and the podium, my parents had set up two long tables with food, food warmers, dessert, and a three-level cake, which seemed oddly out of place.

My mother looked beautiful in her long blue dress. To please her, I wore a long red one. I felt ridiculous, but I wanted my grandfather to have a special celebration. I was surprised to see my father wearing a suit. He said my mother had insisted, and he didn't want to raise her blood pressure more than it already was.

Every corner of the house exuded the holiday spirit. Snowmen, reindeer, Santa Clauses, and sleighs sprinkled all around the house in a festive array—of reds, greens, and whites—filled me with joy.

The doorbell rang around 4 p.m. when my parents were in the backyard finalizing the last details, so I opened the door and saw Uncle Julio, his wife, and his entire family, all nicely dressed in fancy holiday attire. His five children and their significant others accompanied him, as well as four little ones I did not recognize, two girls and two boys.

"Uncle Julio, everyone, I'm so glad you could make it! Please come in," I said, hugging and kissing each person as they entered the house.

I asked them to sit down. My parents had enough space in the formal living and dining rooms for about twenty guests. Dad had installed the extension on the ash wood dining room table so it could accommodate ten people. Julio's children and their spouses sat there, and the four grandchildren sat in the living room next to their grandparents. The two little girls, dressed in cute holiday dresses with matching fancy bows on their hair, noticed my mother's piano and rushed to it. They sat next to each other on the bench and began to touch its keys. I loved seeing them in front of the decorated piano.

Mami had learned how to play when she was a child. She could play by ear and paid for piano lessons for me, but I could never replicate her talent and became frustrated with the lessons.

"Children, come sit next to me. Don't touch the piano," Julio said. Julio was taller and thinner than my father and very handsome, with a square face, thick biceps, and a full head of grey hair. I could see why he had so many children from different women.

"Let them play. Don't worry about it," I said. "So, Uncle Julio, I recognize everyone except for the children and my most recent cousin."

His children started to laugh.

Julio, Jr., Julio's only son with my uncle's Cuban wife Maritza, said, "Lena, this is my half-sister Adaku." He pointed at the beautiful African-American woman.

"Which means 'daughter born into wealth,'" Adaku said. She stood up and shook my hand.

"No hand-shaking here. Cubans give hugs. Besides, we are family. I already hugged you, but here is another one."

She allowed me to embrace her and smiled. "And this is my husband, Thomas. I know what you must be thinking. How can this black woman be my uncle's daughter?"

"Oh no. I don't think that at all. You have his light-brown eyes and some of his facial features. I definitely see the resemblance. Your father has some good genes because all of you look stunning."

They all smiled.

"Can I bring you something to drink?" I asked.

"No, let's wait for the rest of the family to arrive," my uncle suggested.

"Well, let me go to the backyard and tell my parents you are here. I don't think they heard the door."

I rushed to the backyard.

"Mami, Julio, and his family are here. Did you know he had four grandchildren, two little girls, and two little boys?"

"No, he never said anything."

"He must have told you something," I said.

"No, he didn't!" my mother protested.

"Four more guests?" said my father.

"I have no presents for them," my mother replied. "Oh my God. What am I going to do? Alberto, you need to run to the toy store and buy four toys, two for girls and two for boys."

"It's Christmas Day! Are you crazy? There is nothing open! Do you have some bears from when Lena was growing up, or did she take them all home?"

"I may have a couple here," she said. "I can put some money in envelopes for the boys."

"You're giving his grandchildren old bears for Christmas?" I asked.

"What do you want us to do? You hardly played with them anyway. You kept them for decoration," my mother said.

"Whatever, just hurry up. Dad, can you say hello? Was that the bell again?"

It was Maylin's daughter with her husband, their two daughters, and their spouses. Moments later, my grandfather and Tía Rita arrived, then my cousin Marta and her parents, my friend Maggie with her new boyfriend, my parents' coworkers, and finally, the priest. When I saw my cousin, Marta, I asked her, "Have you seen Paulo lately?"

"I'm sorry. I haven't," she replied, but this time, she didn't make the flirtatious face she did when she had spoken about him in the past.

My father moved all the guests to the backyard and asked everyone to sit down. I asked Mamá whether her sister Samantha, who lived in New York, was coming. She said that one of her daughters was sick, and she could not make it.

"Testing, one, two, three. Testing one, two, three," he said, speaking into the microphone. "Can everyone hear me?"

"Yes," a few family members replied.

"My lovely wife wants to make an introduction."

Everyone remained silent and looked at my mother.

"I would like to thank you all for joining us today. It's great to see the family together, almost two years after the pandemic began. Dad wanted to see the family reunited again, and I am glad that we can make his wishes a reality. Before we serve dinner, I would like to have Father Rogelio bless our food and this gathering. After that, we will have a special announcement."

Father Rogelio took the microphone, blessed the gathering and the food, and then returned it to my mother.

"This Christmas will be one to remember," my mother said. "We have so much to be thankful for, but we also have a surprise. Someone very dear to our family is here to sing a Spanish song for our daughter. Lena, you had asked us what your Christmas present was this year, and here it is. Paulo, you can come outside now."

My heart began to beat faster the moment I saw him dressed in a black tuxedo. What was he doing here? I covered my mouth with my hands while all eyes kept switching between Paulo and me. Paulo walked toward the podium and took the microphone, a big smile adorning his expression.

He looked like a movie star, from his assertive walk to the eyes I adored.

"Hello, everyone; before I make the announcement, I would like to sing a song to Lena, a song that conveys how I feel, how I have always felt about her. I would like to thank her grandfather for teaching it to me. We have been working on this performance for several days. He will play the guitar. Sir, would you do me the honor?"

My grandfather walked toward Paulo, gleaming with joy, and grabbed his guitar. My father brought him a chair and accommodated a portable microphone on his tie.

"This is for you, Lena," Paulo said.

He then began to sing the Spanish love song *Bésame Mucho.*

When I heard the lyrics, "Kiss me, kiss me a lot, as if this were our last night, I fear to love you, and lose you then," my eyes filled with tears, and before I could help it, my emotions rolled down my face. The moment he noticed my reddened face, he spread his arms, and I walked toward him. He couldn't finish the song because we lost each other in a long-overdue embrace while my grandfather wiped a tear.

As if I had not received enough surprises for one day, Paulo dropped to one knee and held my hand. Everyone stood up and applauded when they saw him. In his hand, I noticed the ring, "Lena, will you marry me today?"

"Today?"

I glanced at my parents. They were both embracing and holding hands.

"Did you know?" I asked my mother.

She nodded and wiped the tears that had managed to escape from her eyes.

"Well, will you take me as your husband? If you do, I promise to love you and care for you for the rest of my life."

"Yes! I do! Oh my God. I can't believe it! I can't believe it!"

He stood up and hugged me, and kissed my lips. Moments later, from among the crowd, a man I didn't recognize emerged and walked toward us. He wore a suit, had gray hair, and the deep wrinkles of someone who had suffered too much.

"Lena, this is my father, Christiano Oliviera."

I glanced at both of them, perplexed. "But how?"

"I'll explain shortly."

I hugged his father, and Papi brought him another chair so he could sit next to my grandfather.

The priest approached the podium again.

"By the way, Paulo, I never said you could kiss the bride," the priest said.

Paulo giggled and apologized. Father Rogelio took the microphone again and began our wedding ceremony.

The priest recited a few verses from the Bible and then said that Paulo had written a letter he wanted to read to me. Paulo unfolded a couple of pages he had in his pants pocket, connected the microphone my grandfather handed him to his lapel, and began to read:

Dear Lena,

So much has happened since I received your letter almost three months ago that I have decided to condense these events into a letter. Hopefully, this will be the second and last letter between us, two letters that our children will be able to read when neither of us is here.

Shortly after yours arrived, I received a call from a childhood friend who had grown up with me in the favela.

"Gangs have taken your father hostage. They are asking for $50,000 in ransom for his safe return. You need to come to Brazil right away."

I had no choice but to speak with your grandfather and your dad to explain what was happening. They advised me against going back to Brazil, given the current situation with crime and gangs. The pandemic has only made things worse, but I did what I had to do. They agreed to keep an eye on my business.

I hired a group of armed security guards upon my arrival in São Paulo, and we began searching for my father. I had already lost my brother to gang violence, and I wasn't about to lose him, too. The gang leader had asked me to bring the ransom money with me, but I knew he would have simply kept the money and killed my father and me. I had to make it difficult for the gang to get to the money, but that also meant risking my life.

I was finally able to find my father and, with the help of the United States Embassy in Sao Paulo, get him out of Brazil with a temporary visa. My attorney thinks we have a good case, given that returning my father to Brazil would be a death sentence for him.

When I was back in Brazil, walking through dark alleys in search of my father, thinking that I would not live to tell my story, the thought of you illuminated my path. You must know that if the world were to end a month from now, I would die happy if I could get to spend the last days of my life with you. You are my blue skies. I love you, Lena.

As I start a new life with you, I promise to raise our family within the traditions of both of our parents. Our children will be Cuban, Brazilian, and North American. They will learn what is possible through love, family, and hard work. This is my commitment to you.

I may not be a college-educated man, but I will work hard for you and our family to give you the life you deserve.

Yours always,

Paulo

When I glanced around the yard, I noticed happy tears. My mother was right. This would be the most memorable Christmas of our lives. Before I had a chance to say anything, the priest began to speak again, but I told him I, too, had a few words to say. The words sprouted from my mouth as if I had rehearsed them. I could not believe it.

"My love, in front of my family, God, and those who I hope are watching from heaven—your mom, my grandmother Matilda, your brother, and my Nana Maylin—I commit myself to loving you and to never allow anything or anyone to separate us. I promise to fight for you with all of my being and to care for you until the last day of my life. From my grandfather's letters, I learned to follow my heart. It has a strange way of telling us where happiness awaits."

Joy radiated from Paulo's eyes and mine, and while holding hands and locking gazes, we listened to the words of the priest.

"Do you, Paulo Oliveira, take Lena Pérez to be your lawfully wedded wife, to have and to hold from this day forward, for better, for worse, for richer, for poorer, in sickness and in health, until death do you part?"

"I do."

"Do you, Lena Pérez, take Paulo Oliveira to be your lawfully wedded husband, to have and to hold from this day forward, for better, for worse, for richer, for poorer, in sickness and in health, until death do you part?"

"I do."

"By the power vested in me by the Catholic Church, I now declare you husband and wife. You may kiss the bride."

MEMORIES AND LETTERS FROM CUBA

Becky Lima

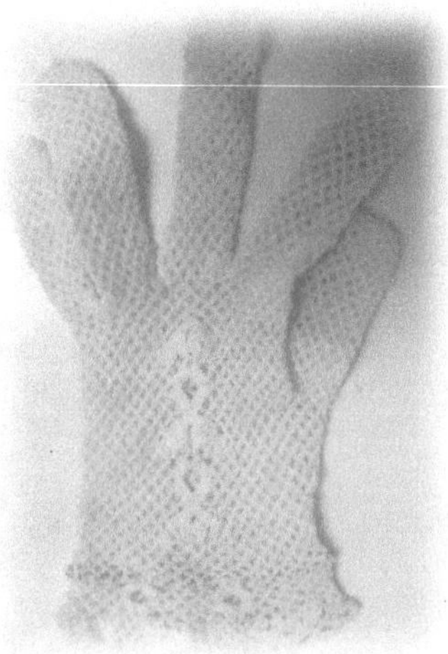

Becky was nine in 1961 when her mother sent her and her sister alone to the United States through the Pedro Pan Operation. Becky was wearing this glove. She lost the other while on the plane, which would bring her to freedom. In her small purse, her mother had placed the items shown in the next few pages. The note in the religious stamp on the next page reads:

My precious little Becky, look at Jesus so he will care for you. See how handsome he looks. Notice his little face, just like yours. You looked a lot like that precious face. He is beautiful, isn't he?

Mi Bequita presiosa mira
bién a Jesus, que lindo
para que te cuide mucho
mira su carita, así eras tu
de veras, te parecías mucho
a esa presiosa carita;
Es lindisimo verdad.

01130

Copyright 1939 N. G. Boseri

Para Bequita

Recuerdo

de la

Primera Comunión

del niño

Luis P. Hernández

Sosa

efectuada en la

Capilla del Asilo Arca

el día 1 de Junio de 1961

Cienfuegos

Memories of Becky's first communion on June 1, 1961

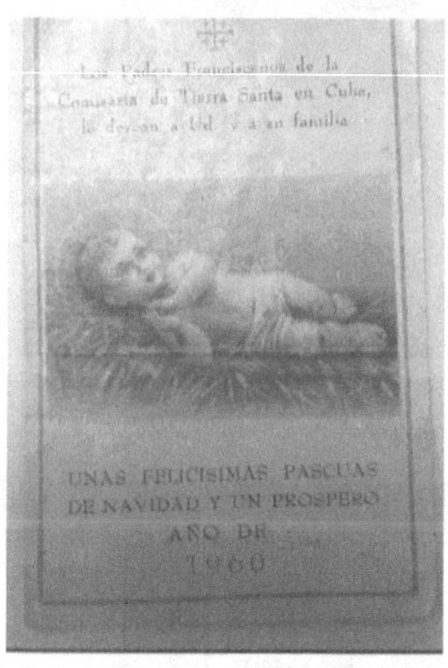

Los Padres Franciscanos de la Comisaría de Tierra Santa en Cuba, le desean a Ud. y a su familia

UNAS FELICISIMAS PASCUAS DE NAVIDAD Y UN PROSPERO AÑO DE 1960

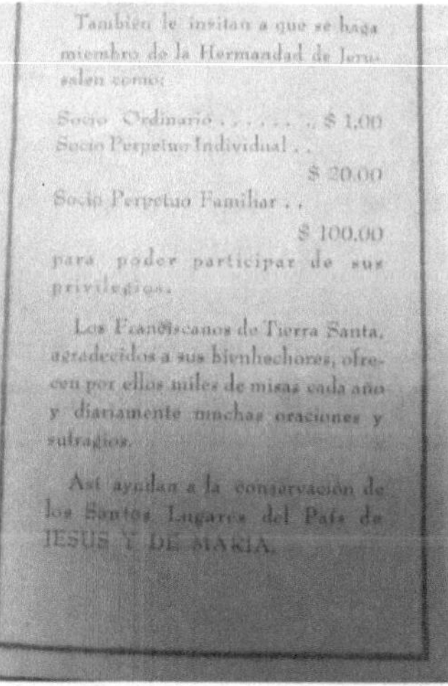

También le invitan a que se haga miembro de la Hermandad de Jerusalen como:

Socio Ordinario . . . . $ 1.00
Socio Perpetuo Individual . .
$ 20.00
Socio Perpetuo Familiar . .
$ 100.00

para poder participar de sus privilegios.

Los Franciscanos de Tierra Santa, agradecidos a sus bienhechores, ofrecen por ellos miles de misas cada año y diariamente mnchas oraciones y sufragios.

Así ayudan a la conservación de los Santos Lugares del País de JESUS Y DE MARIA.

Christmas religious stamp from the church to Becky's family in 1960

Rosa Maria Llerena

These are some of the postcards that her brother sent her in 1962 within her mother's letters. She was the youngest and the only girl of four siblings. She came to the United States on May 21, 1962, at age 13, through the Pedro Pan Operation and stayed at Our Lady of Lourdes Nogales foster home in Arizona. Her oldest brother, José, had to stay in Cuba with his parents. He was finally able to leave the island on February 28, 1965, via Spain. However, during the years the siblings spent apart, José always sent his sister postcards so she could feel the love of her family despite the physical distance.

Today, in 2021, Rosa—in her 70s—lives in a condominium in Hollandale Beach next to her brother José. Her other siblings have died. She feels

Picture of Rosa Maria and her older brother

that life or fate has always had a way of keeping her brother and her together, despite it all.

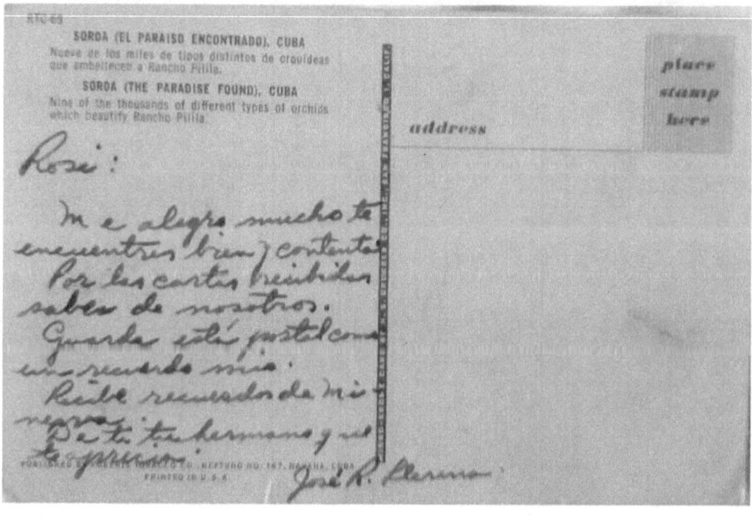

RTC-69

SOROA (EL PARAISO ENCONTRADO), CUBA

Nueve de los miles de tipos distintos de orquídeas que embellecen a Rancho Pilila.

SOROA (THE PARADISE FOUND), CUBA

Nine of the thousands of different types of orchids which beautify Rancho Pilila.

address

place stamp here

Rosi:

Me alegro mucho te encuentres bien y contenta. Por las cartas recibidas sabes de nosotros. Guarda esta postal como un recuerdo mío. Recibe recuerdos de mi negra. De tu hermano y que te aprecia.

José R. Llerena

PRINTED IN U.S.A.

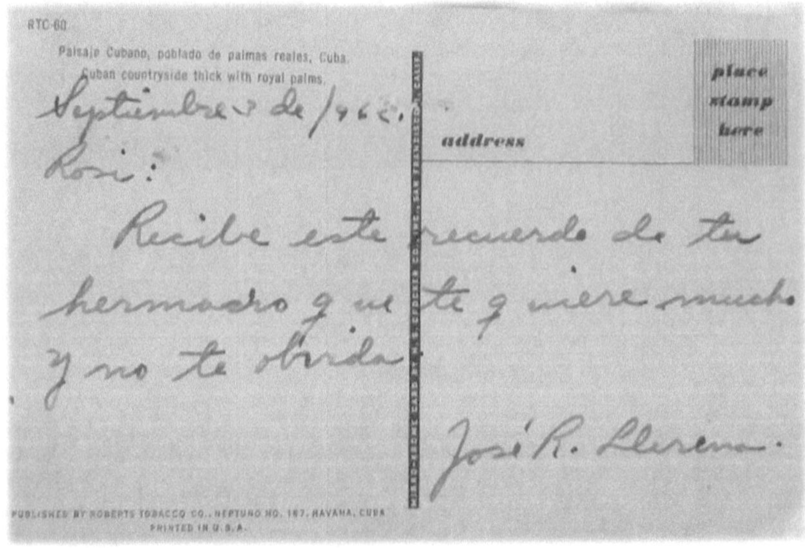
RTC-60

Paisaje Cubano, poblado de palmas reales, Cuba.
Cuban countryside thick with royal palms.

Septiembre 3 de 1962.

Rosi:

Recibe este recuerdo de tu hermanito que te quiere mucho y no te olvida.

José R. Llerena.

address

place stamp here

PUBLISHED BY ROBERTS TOBACCO CO., NEPTUNO NO. 167, HAVANA, CUBA
PRINTED IN U.S.A.

Jane Marie Haney (aka Juana Maria Aragon-Rodriguez).

This letter is from Juama Maria Aragon's mother:

RECEIVED
MAR 17 1964

Sister Mary Elizabeth
Superior
Catholic Children's Home
Illinois.

Dear Sister: Some time ago a cousin of Juanita called Teresita Aragon asked me let Juanita go with her but it was as only to spend a month with them, by that time I get a letter from you explaining to me it was impossible let Juanita go unless her cousin take her. Well my dear Sister I wish tell you my niece Teresita wrote me a very nice letter asking we let her and to her husband take Juanita Maria with them and she wrote that they will be like her own parent, they love very much to my dear girl and I see my travel is very far yet that is what I wish ask you let Juanita go with them. Teresita wrote me Juanita will be the same as their little boys, and her husband will be very happy to have my girl with them; I know it's truth. So I ask you when Teresita wishes let Juanita go, I never could forget how kind you have been for her, there's no gold in all the world to pay you what you have dome with her, I hope God will let me some day go where you are to give thank you. My heart is full of love for you dear Sister, believe me, I could not forget who was sokind and sweet with my dear girl, the same happen with her housemother, teachers and all person who was near of Juanita; All my life will be remembering Sister Gilbert, Alfrida, Williams, everybody who help to Juanita in every way. You be sure I feel a little of sadness thinking of taking out her, but I wish she go with her family because she is forgetting all about her family and besides I don't know when I will go; I'm sure Teresita will care her very much, and you be sure Juanita always remember you; that's all Sister, my english is very poor I have not a lot of words to express what I feel in my heart, but know all what I tell you is truth.

Remember us in your prayer, we need it very much, and you my dear Sister receive my sincerely love. Your friend

signed: Caridad Rodrigues

Jane's mother passed away in February 2021. After her death, she found a letter that her mother sent from Cuba to Sister Mary Elizabeth from the Catholic Children's Home in Illinois on March 17, 1964, when she realized she would not be able to reunite with her daughter as soon as she had originally thought. In it, she thanked the Catholic Church for all it had done for her daughter and explained that she had decided to allow her daughter to live with family, as she was afraid the girl would forget about them.

The Ring

My paternal grandmother was given a diamond ring on her fifteenth birthday. She had two sons. So, after I was born, she told my parents that when I turned fifteen, she was going to pass her ring on to me.

In January 1959, all our lives changed when Fidel Castro came to power.

In October 1961, my parents, my sisters, my maternal grandparents, and I left Cuba and came to the United States. However, my paternal grandparents and uncle stayed behind because my uncle had bought into the false promises of Castro's revolution. He was ten years younger than my father, unmarried, and my grandparents didn't want to leave him alone.

In 1970, I turned fifteen. My paternal grandmother wrote a letter to my parents explaining that she was sending me a special card in celebration of this occasion. The letter stated that she didn't want me to miss my "recuerdo" for my fifteenth birthday.

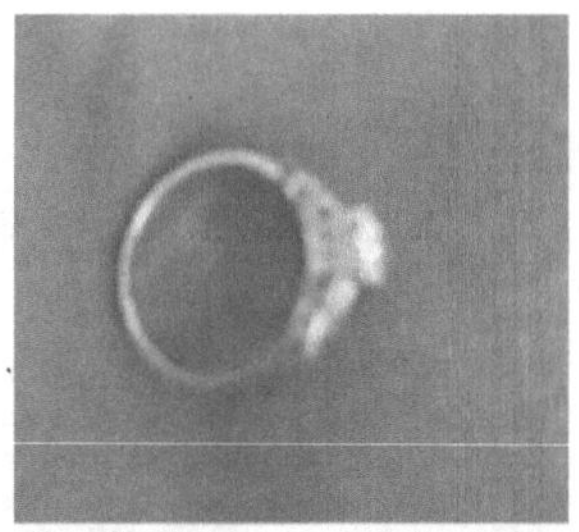

My card arrived about a week later. It was home-made and had a little padded section. My parents studied it, as they had read between the lines of her previous letter. My dad warned me not to get upset, but he planned to open up the pad.

I did get upset! I didn't want my card destroyed. Besides, I didn't know anything about the ring. As carefully as possible, my dad opened it up. And there, hidden in the padding, was my grandmother's beautiful ring!

Conchita Hicks

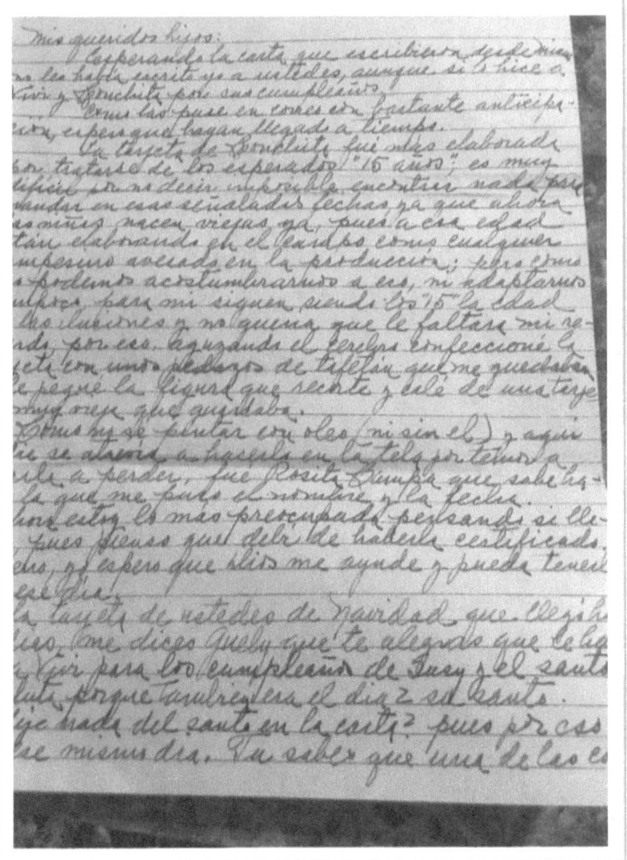

Mis queridos hijos:
Esperando la carta que escribieron desde Miami no les había escrito yo a ustedes, aunque sí le hice a Vivi y Conchita por sus cumpleaños.
Como las puse en correo con bastante anticipación, espero que hayan llegado a tiempo.

Excerpt from the letter (translated from Spanish).

February 26, 1970

My dear children,

I had not written to you because I was waiting for the letter you wrote from Miami, although I did write to Vivi and Conchita for their birthdays.

I mailed them well in advance, and I hope they arrived on time.

Conchita's card was more elaborate because it was her "fifteenth birthday." It is very difficult, if not impossible, to find anything to send, as girls grow up so quickly, often having to work in the fields at an early age, just like seasoned farmers. However, I cannot get used to that or adapt to it. For me, they are still fifteen, the age of illusions, and I did not want "my gift" to be missing, so after thinking about what to do, I made the card with some pieces of taffeta I found, and I glued a figure I cut from a very old card.

As I do not know how to paint with oil (or without it), and here nobody dares to do it on canvas for fear of spoiling them, it was Rosita Campa who knows how to do it, who drew the name and the date.

Now I'm most worried about whether it will arrive on time. Maybe I should have sent it via certified mail.

Well, I hope God helps me, and Conchita can have it on that special day.

I love you all very much.

Nenita

Dr. Pastor Alayo Dalmau

Dr. Pastor Alayo Dalmau was a graduate of the University of Santiago and a Road Scholar. He also wrote the only book that contained all of Cuba's butterflies, which was entitled *Atlas de las mariposas diurnas de Cuba (Lepidoptera, Rhopalocera)*. Not only was he one of the most transcendental Cuban naturalists, but he was also the godfather of the award-winning documentary producer and screenwriter Manny Soto, who submitted these postcards painted by this influential man for inclusion in this book. Dr. Pastor Alayo Dalmau passed away in 2001, but his works have endured. Like letters, the book Dr. Pastor Alayo Dalmau wrote, and these postcards are droplets of life that remind us of the beauty that surrounds us, that sometimes we don't stop to enjoy.

A Letter from Ramona

On July 11, 2021, the Cuban people, tired of the inhumane conditions and repression within Cuba, poured into the streets to demand freedom. Both young and old chanted "*Libertad*," "*Abajo con Diaz-Canel*," "*Cubanos Unidos jamás serán vencidos*," and "*Patria y Vida*."

They were asking for liberty, the removal of the unelected "President" Diaz-Canel, unity, and homeland and life. In addition to the lack of freedom, Cubans had to spend hours in line to buy whatever goods came to the stores that day; they lacked medicine and basic personal care products; when they went to hospitals, they had to bring sheets and their food; and many were dying without medical attention because of a collapsed hospital system.

The response from their government was immediate:

1. A threatening speech at 4 p.m. on Sunday, July 11, 2021, encouraging "revolutionaries" to fight with the protestors
2. Removal of the Internet
3. Electricity was shut down for several hours that evening. It had always been intermittent on the island. However, with extreme shortages and uncontrolled inflation, Cubans could not risk their limited food supplies in the refrigerator spoiling due to a lack of power. Additionally, the elderly, under the unbearable heat of the summer months, could not even turn on a fan during the prolonged power outages.

More drastic measures were implemented on the following days when buses full of government men carrying sticks and appearing to be professionally trained were deployed in Havana to beat up the peaceful protestors. Police and the military were also going house to house searching for protestors. Plainclothes police and military were deployed throughout the island, as well as the feared "Boinas Negras," a highly trained group of men.

Hundreds of protestors disappeared in only a few hours.

In many European countries and the United States, people took to the streets in support of the protesters.

Five days after the protests started, I received this letter via e-mail from a relative in Cuba. It was July 16, 2021:

Dear Betty,

I have seen your Facebook posts, and I like them, but everything is going to stay the same. The government was surprised by the massive protests. Yet, they have also learned a valuable lesson. From now on, they will become more ruthless because they now know that the people of Cuba are not the same as they were twenty years ago and that they must treat them differently. They are also AFRAID that another phenomenon like the one that occurred on the 11th will recur.

Notice that the police are everywhere on the street, and some are wearing plain clothes. So, I ask you a question: Who in Cuba is going to go anywhere? People may know that they can protest, but nothing more.

I knew that the waters would level very quickly and that nothing would be achieved. We were appeased with a piece of candy. It was like giving a dog a treat.

Now, travelers who come can bring food, medicines, and other products. Oh, how good is the Revolution! How loving it is to the people!

Those in charge are rats, and we continue to fall into their traps.

Betty, this is the reality, and nothing has happened here. I repeat, I am sorry for the Cubans who remain on the streets and demonstrate in support of us. They are getting excited and fighting for nothing. After all, everything around us will remain the same.

Homeland and Life!

Love,

Ramona

Picture of demonstrations in support of the Cuban people living on the island who risked their lives in the name of freedom. Taken in Tampa, Florida on July 11, 2021

The Cuban Poet

On the evening of September 9, 2021, I received a letter from a poet in Cuba. She had been reading my posts and wanted to tell me how she felt about the conditions on the island.

Our discussion impacted me. I imagined what it was like to be denied one's true history. I also knew what it was like not to be able to express oneself freely.

We exchanged several messages over the next few days.

She had been born in a fishermen's town, Batabanó, where my mother had taken me when I was a child, and I had fond memories of this place. My mother wanted us to see the town, and she had taken several buses to get us there. By the time we arrived, my siblings and I were hungry, thirsty, and tired. My mother didn't have much money, so she approached one of the fishermen's boats and asked if they could cook some fresh fish for us and give us some water. I was shocked at her audacity, but years later, I would understand what a desperate mother could do.

She then did what she always did: tell the fishermen that the Cuban government was keeping our family (a mother and her three children) separated from my father, who lived in the United States.

The fishermen must have felt pity for my mother and invited us into their boat. They made us rice and fresh fish, the most delicious fish I had ever tasted.

My encounter with the poet brought me these memories so vividly. She sent me a couple of poems. She wanted to gift them to me, but I told her that I would publish one of them in my book and give her the appropriate credit. Here is the translation. She allowed me to give her poem a title, as it didn't have one. For fear of being jailed, she used a pen name.

The cry of my Cuba

No more crying, no more pain
No more nights of blackouts
No more hatred and heartbreak
Nor laws that cut like blades.

No more imposed shortages
of medicine and food
and abuses that now stink.
Cubans, don't let them oppress you
Don't let their blows break you
Rise proudly and walk.

Place your courage first.
With justice from the heavens.
If David defeated Goliath
God will provide you with great comfort
Of the shining star
in your flag and on your soil

This poem was written by Ester Reina (A Cuban poet currently residing in Cuba – translated by Betty Viamontes). Fearing for her safety, she provided a pen name.

***

Letters are like droplets of life, snapshots of moments that won't return.

Acknowledgments

I would like to thank the following individuals and organizations:

All the people who submitted their testimonies for inclusion in this book.

Becky Lima de Arce for all her help and support.

Susana Mueller, from Susanabooks, for designing a superb book cover and for being a beta reader for this manuscript.

Conchita Hicks, another beta reader, provided valuable comments about the manuscript.

To the Facebook group *All Things Cuban* for providing an important forum for the dissemination of Cuban history and culture. Alexander Diaz, thank you!

To my husband Ivan for making suggestions about various chapters of this book. His contributions have been invaluable. To my mother-in-law Madeline, my son Ivan and his wife Gloria, my brother Rene, and my sister Lissette for their contributions.

To the group *Women Reading Great Books* for their suggestions regarding the cover.

Acknowledgments

To all the readers who continue to support me and share my posts and all the book clubs that have selected my books, too many to mention.

Warhistory.com for the following article: The 4 Month Long Battle for Support Station Ripcord (warhistoryonline.com)

Vietnam 40 years later: 101st Airborne Division veteran recalls Ripcord battle Article, The United States Army

Cuba history.org - Special Period and Recovery

Other Works by the Author

Betty's stories have traveled the world, from the award-winning *Waiting on Zapote Street* to the No. 1 new releases *The Girl from White Creek* and *The Pedro Pan Girls: Seeking Closure.*

Other works include:

Brothers: A Pedro Pan Story

Havana: A Son's Journey Home

The Dance of the Rose

Under the Palm Trees: Surviving Labor Camps in Cuba

Candela's Secrets and Other Havana Stories

Like Finding Water in the Desert (a collaboration between four authors)

The above books are available in English and Spanish. *Waiting on Zapote Street* was one of the winners of The Latino Books Into Movies award and has been selected by a United Nations women's book club and many others.

Betty's works have appeared in various publications, including the prestigious literary journal *The Mailer Review*. Betty's goal is to ensure that the stories of the Cuban people are not forgotten and to give a voice to people who don't have one.

www.ingramcontent.com/pod-product-compliance
Lightning Source LLC
LaVergne TN
LVHW090952080826
845145LV00003B/977

* 9 7 8 1 9 5 5 8 4 8 0 4 6 *